To: Doug & Joan,

FISSURE ROCK

Thanks for coming out! Happy reading!

John Blair
☺

FISSURE ROCK

John Blair

Copyright © 2003 by John Blair.

Library of Congress Number: 2003095137
ISBN : Hardcover 1-4134-2254-3
       Softcover 1-4134-2253-5

All rights reserved. No part of this book may be reproduced or transmitted in any form or by any means, electronic or mechanical, including photocopying, recording, or by any information storage and retrieval system, without permission in writing from the copyright owner.

This is a work of fiction. Names, characters, places and incidents either are the product of the author's imagination or are used fictitiously, and any resemblance to any actual persons, living or dead, events, or locales is entirely coincidental.

This book was printed in the United States of America.

To order additional copies of this book, contact:
Xlibris Corporation
1-888-795-4274
www.Xlibris.com
Orders@Xlibris.com
20174

I dedicate this book
in loving memory to my hero,
my father,
Donald F. Blair

ACKNOWLEDGEMENTS

For their editorial help, I thank the following folks in my native Toronto, Canada:

Bill Belfontaine
Sharon Crawford (and the East End Writers' Group)
Avery Hurtig
Fraser Mitchell
David Read

And to my New Jersey friends, who gave me their helpful advice and encouragement:

Addison Cooper
Jim Vivanco

ROCK ONE

HERE WE ARE, the fearless family foursome zooming down this rural highway thanks to Dad's penchant for high speeds. Mom says nothing. In fact no one's spoken a word since our lunch stop an hour ago. My younger sister Lisa has Walkman plugs glued into her ears which is, believe me, a good thing. The end-of-summer sun is blazing and all four windows have been rolled right down; it's not hot enough to click on the air conditioner.

We're getting closer. From the back seat of Dad's beloved five-year-old gold Malibu (I'm hoping to get my beginner's license soon now that I'm 16), my eyes decipher the black lettering etched on an off-green sign just before it whizzes past. "Fissure Rock, population: 10,000," I announce.

Beside me a perpetually sarcastic voice pipes up. "Oh, yay, the boy can read," she snipes before returning to the sounds blasting into her eardrums.

Naturally I can't allow her insulting comments to evaporate unrewarded. Using a pleasant tone that always manages to irritate her, I egg her on. "Shame. Now they'll have to change it to read: 10,004."

She stares into the back of Mom's head while bitterly suggesting, "Or we could go back home where we belong and save these crazy country hicks a lotta time and money."

Waving my index finger, I smile at her freckled scowl and brown frizzled hair. "Something tells me you're not in too good a mood."

"Shut up, Jimmy!" Lisa doesn't like it when I smile; life's supposed to be incurably crappy.

Dad butts in. "Now, honey," he draws out, "you know your

brother doesn't appreciate being called Jimmy anymore." Poor Dad never knows when to leave well enough alone.

"How about moron, then?" my sister shouts back with all the venom only a fourteen-year-old brat can muster. Her increased vocabulary impresses me.

Mom's traveling voice is usually a whisper. "Actually Bill, you could slow down a little. We're closing in on civilization now." The nervousness is showing through.

Dad lets up slightly on the accelerator, which gives me more time to look directly out my left window at the scenery surrounding the town of what will be our new home. Large mounds of cracked granite rock are mixed with sun-bleached carpets of yellow September grass hugging the roadside. Beyond that there is a forbidding forest. My glance to the right is blocked by Lisa's stubborn noise-filled head. By leaning forward I see the landscape gives way to human habitation. I catch a tiny combination grocery store/gas bar nestled between medium-sized trees. But the most significant feature is the uneven rock surface. There must have been miniature streams and waterfalls a few centuries ago, leaving behind all these solid creases on the surface and in granite walls. In some places, the jagged rock is twenty feet high. The feeling is eerie, like riding through a maze of tunnels. It's good luck I don't get claustrophobia.

Hard to believe my Dad's pushing fifty. He has a full head of hair, going gray, but his lean body is kept in shape by a daily rigorous routine of jogging and stomach crunches. I used to be his exercise partner until last year when I decided I was just too old to be tagging along with my father—someone from school might see me!

Back in the city, Dad's newspaper advertising job became "redundant." This happened once the new owners discovered freelance advertisers, who work on limited-time contracts, are a lot less expensive in the long run. So after fifteen years there, Dad was given a meager severance pay and a crappy send-off: a 'best wishes Bill' card signed by everyone in the office. He treasures that card as something profoundly meaningful. However, I know, as far as those paper people are concerned, Bill Bridgeman is insignificant compared to their garish headlines. He's yesterday's news, his time has expired, and a history of loyal duties is easily forgotten.

Anyway our family often camped at Fissure Rock when Lisa and I were so young neither one of us remembers anymore. My father's big plan was for the whole family to move up here. Fresh air, good old-fashioned small town values—all that stuff. He's a bit of a dreamer. Still his optimism is contagious, and I was well infected when he presented his proposal to us. Yeah, I thought as if trapped in a trance, this will be a "happy, exciting life-altering experience," just like he said. Besides I've always loved the country. Maybe I'll have a better chance of finding a girlfriend up here.

Lisa fought the idea like she was being attacked by sharks, but we've learned to expect this behaviour from her about, well, everything. My parents believe it's the girl-to-woman phase she's going through. They don't know about Gerald.

Following Dad's original brainstorm, fireworks flew, bursting into the sky. First the house was sold. How stupid is that? I mean, shouldn't they have waited and found a new one in town? There was a mad scramble at the last minute. Finally they bought the house we're on our way to now. Two days before Dad landed local employment, Mom got a job at the town library. A building filled with books will suit her fine. I figure the only thing she loves more than reading is clinging to us like beautifully flowered wallpaper.

Mom's well preserved for a forty-five year old. I used to cringe when my friends would confide in me about her. Do you really want your buds referring to your own mother as "hot?" I know I don't. Like me she's got pale green eyes and wavy blonde hair, medium in length. It's almost impossible to guess what's on her mind, and a long time ago I gave up trying to read her facial expression or body language. None of us has any inkling how she really feels about this move. She might love the change; she might hate it.

"Oh, my God." This is Lisa's negative reaction to a huge sign warning readers, 'Prepare to Meet Thy Lord!' I guess 'Welcome to Fissure Rock' just doesn't pack the same punch as Dad's Malibu cruises down the main street, which is cluttered with shops and tiny offices on both sides. Sunday . . . guess that's why there's not many people around.

Dad parks in front of the Sacalla Real Estate office. "Okay, gang, I'm just going to get the keys from Sally." Dad pops out of the car like a jubilant jack-in-the-box.

While we wait in silence I look around at the handful of people on the sidewalk and elsewhere. Across the street an almost deserted parking lot spreads out from a run-down restaurant. Some kids about my age are hanging out, skateboarding, smoking, swearing. I'm not crazy about boarding and the stink of cigarette smoke makes me want to puke. That's not to say I don't enjoy anything other than reading and writing. Swimming and soccer are what I'm into. Older people also waddle by trying to hide their curious looks. Lisa stares back defiantly. Mom and I smile, as we're more the neighbourly types. Already I'm fitting in with the slow pace of this town.

Dad emerges from the real estate office, bopping along, accompanied by a woman about Mom's age. Right away you can tell she's got on way too much make-up. "Hello, Bridgemans!" she sings through the open window on my side, waving her hand from where the keys jingle. Her breath hints of alcohol, but she's got charm and is holding herself together with great confidence. We already know this woman is Sally Sacalla; Dad feels the need to do the introductions regardless. Kind of neat to see him so happy. Back in the city, after losing his job, he roamed about the house like someone searching for a bottle of pills to end it all. I can't help feeling happy for him, for all of us. Sally hired Dad to do all her advertising. That'll give him the start he needs.

OKAY, SO NOW WE'RE UNPACKING BOXES in our new house. The furniture arrived ahead of us yesterday, and it's the first project Dad and I tackle with Mom telling us, "This goes here" and "That goes there." My sister, whining all the way of course, exaggerates about having to take things up to her room seventeen or more times. "Why didn't you tell me when I was down here, before?" While my parents and I are wearing shorts and light tops, Lisa sweats it out in a pair of blue overalls and a sweatshirt that are both a size too big and she complains that it's cold. Maybe if she worked as hard as the rest of us she'd warm up.

Taking extra care I prop up my acoustic guitar in a corner of my bedroom. Suddenly I remember our cat, Sideline. I called him that for the single black stripe running along the right side of his white-and-gray fur. He would've loved trying to hide inside all these empty boxes. Before we moved Mom gave him to the old couple next door.

We're located on a quiet little street (4 Ducksback Drive to be exact) in the southeast part of town. The house is 20 years older and slightly smaller than what we left in the city. With plenty of wood interior it oozes fresh country smells. Winding its way up a short flight of stairs to end on the second floor is an intricately handcrafted railing. Some awesome work went into this place.

My sister gets angry. "This whole thing is crazy!"

We do our best to either humour or simply ignore Lisa's opposition to everything. That's not always so easy to do and even Mom has her limits. "Fine! It may seem crazy to you and if that's the case, young lady, keep your nasty feelings to yourself! I've had enough of all this bellyaching from you!"

Pretending to search through boxes for something else to put away, I'm thinking, 'Way to go, Mom!' It's real rare for her to open fire.

Dad decides to add his fatherly line, "If you're not part of the solution, Lisa, you're part of the problem. Remember that." He smiles at her, hoping she'll smile back. No luck.

Instead something really strange happens. Lisa clenches her fists against her hips, glares at Dad, goes red in the face and virtually screams into his eyes, "No! Why don't you remember that!" She explodes upstairs and we can practically hear and see thunder and lightning storming out of her head as she stomps on each step. Her bedroom door slams shut and I wonder, 'Wow, what's up with that?' I don't like it when my heart races.

Mom continues arranging and rearranging things in the house, with much less enthusiasm. She's trying to hide her upset nerves.

I feel sorry for her and put my arm around her shoulder. "S'okay, Mom."

Gently freeing herself from my grip, she softly breaks her heavy silence, "She's probably worried about school tomorrow and making new friends."

"Yeah," I say in steady support, except Lisa didn't have any old friends back home, unless you want to count a couple of losers she used to hang out with.

Dad, frozen in the middle of the dining room floor, says nothing. He's in a state of shock.

BY 11:30 P.M. I'm sitting up in bed, reading from the small pamphlet Sally Sacalla gave to Dad that details historic Fissure Rock. I learn I was right about water having been here when the town was settled over two hundred years ago. The first European, with his family and friends, dubbed the place Fissure Rock Falls. Originally this was a village of one of the First Nations' tribes, but the printed material doesn't disclose what they had called their living space. Situated three miles north of here next to a lake, the town was moved south beside a river by the European invaders. Years afterwards this waterway somehow disappeared, explaining today's dry surface.

It really bugs me knowing my ancestors barged their way through North America completely uninvited by the native people. I feel guilty over that and about all the starving people around the world. I even feel guilty that I can't do anything to cheer Lisa up (I try to and always fail). Guess you could say 'guilty' is my middle name.

"Anybody home?" Dad strolls in through my half-opened door.

"Hey, a visitor." I put down the brochure.

He chuckles, scans the unpacked boxes and general chaos. "Looks like your old room already."

"You're a real funny guy."

Dad stands there with his hands in his pockets, wondering what to say next. This is just like him. Then he looks me in the eye and says, "Listen, Jim," and takes a deep breath.

I'm waiting. Nothing. His eyes study the pile of books on the floor. I feel like a man left hanging, still alive, and with every swing in the breeze choking me further I'm trying to say, 'Yeah?' (swoosh), 'Yeah?' (swoosh), 'Yeah?'

Finally he spits it out, "Are you all right with tomorrow? First day of school and all?" He looks up from the carpet and goes on, "You know, all this has been so sudden, and it's really agitated your sister."

I bail him out again. "Don't worry, Dad. Everything agitates Lisa, but me? I'm looking forward to school."

"You're sure? I mean, leaving your friends behind—"

He wants to go somewhere I don't. Like the best way to move on is to forget about the past, right? "Dad, I'm glad we're here. It'll be a good change. How are you doin'?"

"That's what I like about you, Jim. Most 16-year-old kids wouldn't give a rat's ass about how their fathers are feeling." We both laugh for a moment. "I dunno, maybe your sister was absolutely right when she called this my selfish mid-life crisis. At times I wish I had your clever head on these stupid shoulders of mine."

"Dad." I hate it when he does that and he does it a lot lately, insisting Mom and me are wonderful, and he's such a failure and doesn't deserve us. I've noticed he never pulls this when Lisa is around. He doesn't really want someone to agree with him.

"Well," he concludes whatever it's all been about by clasping his hands together. "Maybe you'll make the swim team this year. It is a smaller school."

I put my hands behind my head and stretch out on the bed. "Just call me Flipper."

He thinks that's hilarious and laughs again. Then stopping, eyes concentrating on his shoes, voice softer, "Good night, Flipper."

"Later, big guy," I say. And he's gone, closing the door after him; I'm guessing he and Mom want some privacy tonight. I reach up to switch off the light and look out my open window at darkness. A wisp of warm air is tickling the leaves while the odd car rumbles in the distance. It's a perfect night for sleeping. I'm yawning. This has been a long day. As usual I wait for sleep to take me.

Drifting off, I hear a bottle break outside and loud voices. I leap to the open window and see nothing other than different shades of black. Vaguely I can make out a lighter patch that is our backyard and a line of trees. There's a park on the opposite side where the noise is coming from. Since my eyes are useless, I listen intently. All voices are male (I'm assuming around my age), their words indecipherable amidst rattling leaves and crickets adding to the wilderness racket.

Suddenly I hear a yell, "Get him!" Footsteps scramble and grunts are stifled.

Menacing voices repeat the same words: "Yeah, ha-ha! Ha-ha!"

A lone voice begs, "No, no, please don't . . ."

The Get Him voice announces triumphantly, "Body-slam!"

"Ahhhhhhh!"

As the chorus repeats, "Yeah, ha-ha, ha-ha," everything quiets down.

Words are muffled while the group moves slowly away, hushed by brushing leaves and loud insects.

Returning to bed I take a quick glimpse of my clock radio; 1:00 a.m. My stomach flutters. I realize what tomorrow can bring, something I never worried about until now.

ROCK TWO

FISSURE ROCK HIGH SCHOOL is over 100 years old with something like 800 students, compared to the 1600 at my former school. Just about everybody's smoking as I reach the crowded cement stairs at the main entrance. Music pumps out of deafening boom boxes and the kids, yelling and laughing, obviously know each other. Carefully sifting my way through the throng and up the steps, I'm given a few dubious looks. In a way I'm grateful. Being anonymous is way better than becoming instantly known and picked out for some form of abuse. Perfectly cool to chill and size up the situation. After all, I don't know what I'm dealing with here yet. I search for the office to pick up my timetable.

My first class is English. Only two guys are there when I enter; suddenly other students start streaming in. The floors are old hardwood with sawdust smells that put me at ease. Even though the teacher hasn't appeared, the walls are covered with colourful Shakespeare posters as well as comical offbeat cartoons. It's my nature to smile and this cozy classroom really makes me show off the old pearly whites—in a subtle kind of way.

I settle into a seat about three desks from the front. Kids form loose groups in different corners of the room, chatting away, and a few follow my lead by taking their seats. I'm feeling confident as the new guy, granting my head freedom to turn right, left, absorbing whatever's in this place. If I simply sat like a stone and stared at my hands, I'd be labelled as shy. Can't have that.

As all this is going on, she paddles in. Like skilfully steering a canoe she sweeps calmly through a glass lake while frogs on lily pads greet her. The voices, male and female, are all friendly . . .

"Hey!"
"How are you?"

"You look awesome!"

She has straight long flowing blonde hair, ocean-blue eyes, and her fashion-model figure is lost on no one. My guess is this gorgeous girl has been outdoors all summer—great tan! A lifeguard? Maybe she can save me!

The guy sitting beside me says into my right ear, "Want some free advice?"

Quickly looking back I note he's no bigger than my own medium build, so I can't imagine him posing a threat to me. Continuing my stare at the girl in the green summer dress, I answer, "Uh, I guess . . . if it's really free."

"That is the president of our student council. You do not, I repeat, do not want to have anything to do with her."

Because he's spoken with such tremendous conviction, I look at him again. His expression is in fact dead serious. The big round dark eyes don't blink. Voices around us are getting louder.

I return my eyes to her. She joins a standing foursome in light conversation. Sunrays beam through the large antique windows and she's squinting slightly and delicately . . . flawlessly.

"Why?" I whisper. "Is she your girlfriend or what?"

He seems almost horrified by my assumption. "No, thank you." Then he adds, "Ever heard of the female praying mantis?"

This has got to be a prank to be played on the new kid. "Come on, you're not going to compare her to an insect. What's her name, anyway?"

"Trouble. Big Trouble. And here it comes."

She glides down the aisle of desks and has the most cheerful appearance as her eyes twinkle at mine. When she gets to where I'm sitting she glances at the guy who's been talking about her. There's no way she could have heard us. "Hi, Andy. Who's your friend?" Her voice is so pleasant.

Andy doesn't answer, probably because he doesn't know my name yet.

Time to assert myself; I shine my winning smile. "Hi, I'm Jim."

"Great! I'm Cynthia. I always welcome new students to

Fissure." She looks at the doorway where a middle-age man wearing a tie has just walked in carrying a briefcase. "Here comes Mr. King." Cynthia gives me two soft pats on my shoulder. "You'll really like it here, Jim. We'll talk later, okay?"

I smile and nod as she takes her seat. Her very presence has made me feel more alive than usual. Since the teacher is taking ample time unpacking papers and books at his desk, I turn to my seatmate and quip, "So, Andy, that's your idea of trouble, huh?"

He is staring at the chalkboard ahead of him. His voice has a hard edge on it. "Yup. Her and her whole family, man."

WALKING HOME, I keep thinking how fast the day has gone by. Cynthia is only in my first period English class. In-between Science and Math, there's lunch, but I couldn't see her anywhere in the cramped cafeteria. At the end of the day we played basketball in Gym class. That's okay, only I was disappointed by a few things. The school has no pool, so no swimming team. And while gearing up in the locker room, I asked Andy about soccer tryouts. He smiled and shook his head. "It's basketball and football up here. They play hockey and snowboard in winter. There's not much else." He looked like he was going to say something more, but our Gym teacher interrupted and divided us into two teams for basketball. After we hit the court, I figured some of the larger guys would want to foul me (new kid) and they did. I just kept bouncing up and barged right back into the play. No effect!

WE'RE HAVING DINNER when Mom pops Lisa the lethal question about how her day went. She answers with a surly shrug, "School is school, everywhere." No, my sister isn't turning over a new leaf. Not looking up from her plate as she wolfs down today's lasagne, her appetite has been healthy lately. Lisa's pretty good in all subjects at school. Last winter, though, she caught mono and missed too many classes. That's why she has to repeat a grade. I won't need to deal with her existence at FRH for another year . . . Yes!

Dad announces that he'll be doing a fair amount of overtime at his job. "Sally decided to wait until my first day to tell me that our clients come to us at all hours. Many are only part-timers and their work schedules are staggered. Sounds sort of crazy to me."

To this news my mom nods her head. "Today at the library, all I heard was how hard it is for everyone around here to pay their bills."

Dad rallies the troops. "We'll make do. How did your day go, son?"

I almost say: 'Oh, I'm real hot for this blonde girl in a green dress!' However that would be considered too much detail, even rude, especially by my mother. My alternative answer is much more digestible. "Good. I like English class the best."

Mom gives me a scrutinizing look. "You're sure? You feel comfortable in all your subjects?"

"There's no swimming pool but everything else is fine," I assure her.

I'm given an extra-long stare. It's only been like one day. She's way too over-protective.

ROCK THREE

THE WEEK FLIES BY without much special unfolding. Our house is taking shape as all four of us (even Lisa) pitch in to make it look like home inside. At school, Andy and I have lunch together every day. No one joins us. My new friend doesn't seem to be too popular. I don't know why he's been relegated to loner status. He looks okay, not as good looking as me (don't mind my modesty), but he's no mutant either. Twice I catch sight of Cynthia in the cafeteria, with her brood of friends, and from a distance we both smile and wave. I'm anxiously waiting for when "we'll talk later."

From out of nowhere, memories of Brian, Mason and Wendy blitz my brain. Back home, the four of us were best friends. What are my chances up here? When it hurts too much thinking about them—missing them—I stop it.

FRIDAY ROLLS INTO TOWN and Mrs. Kishwar declares a school assembly at high noon. We bring our lunches, sit, and pay attention to the stage area.

"Good afternoon, Fissure students," our principal begins. "As you all know, each academic year we raise money for worthwhile causes. Last year we set a goal of $4,000 for Fissure Rock Hospital and surpassed that amount by reaching close to $6,000. Also, when the hockey team required new equipment your student council was able to acquire the funds necessary through various fundraising activities. We are all aware of the person most responsible for these and similar successes in the name of our school. Your student council president, Cynthia Sacalla."

(Sacalla? Funny, I never knew her last name until this moment.

She must be related to my Dad's boss. Dad's already told us Sally isn't married . . . maybe she's got a niece?)

Healthy applause. Cynthia, in brown slacks and white blouse (school colours), climbs a few steps and on stage shakes hands with the principal. Taking on the poise of a seasoned politician, she approaches the microphone as her host sits down on the steel chair behind her. "Hello fellow Fissurites!" she exclaims with great energy.

I am part of the joyous response, rowdy hand-clapping and foot stomping.

"Thank you, Mrs. Kishwar and all faculty members. This year our local library must have a new building. The current one has many structural problems and suffers floods with each heavy rainfall. We must set our vision on raising sufficient funds to help town council build a modern resource centre with internet access." More cheering voices, including mine, for her finely crafted and delivered speech. "Also, let there be no question about it, by the end of this academic year our school will have enough money to build that swimming pool we've been wanting for so long!"

This vow receives an amazingly favourable reaction, and as you'd expect, I am more than happy. Flipper's going to swim again . . . next year.

Without taking my eyes off Cynthia, I whisper to Andy, "A new swimming pool alone will cost way more than a few thousand dollars."

In his usual matter-of-fact manner, Andy agrees. "She'll raise it, too. All of it, and more." Nothing in his voice offers a trace of admiration for Cynthia's fundraising talents. Exactly the opposite, his tone reveals more contempt for her.

I still don't know what his problem is. I say to him flat out, "Everyone else around here likes her, including me. What is it with you?"

While Cynthia fills in her audience on the many fun activities she has conjured up for getting a new library and swimming pool, Andy keeps his peace. Near the end he says, "If you're smart, you'll remember what I said before."

The cafeteria echoes in a cacophony of clapping hands, whistles, hoots and howls. Cynthia has finished her speech and is returning triumphantly to her table full of friends.

SPECIAL MOMENTS don't happen nearly enough and I guess that's why they're called special moments. My first special moment at Fissure Rock comes in the person of Cynthia. It's weird. I'm thinking about her while I'm walking home, my backpack on my shoulders, and I hear my name being called out. I look back, and guess who it is?

"Jim Bridgeman, your thoughts on week number one at FRH, please?" She's pretending to be a reporter, and the light breeze styles her hair peacefully . . . perfectly.

I have to think before replying. I've enjoyed looking at her in English class, listening to her directing questions at Mr. King and giving him correct answers in return. Everyday I have lunch with Andy (yay, I don't have to eat alone). Other than that the kids have kept their distance. They see me as an outsider. I suppose I can't expect any overnight miracles.

"I'm trying to get the hang of it," I say meekly.

"You'll fit in, don't worry." Her convincing tone makes me believe her right on the spot. "Listen, it's only three-thirty. What a beautiful Friday afternoon! Why don't you come over to my house and we'll do something?"

Talk about being caught off-guard. My forehead is suddenly warm and damp, and the catch in my stomach makes it hard to say anything other than, "Uh, sure."

INSIDE CYNTHIA'S HOUSE I can't escape the sound of a blaring television. She makes a little groan of protest, then raises her voice in a pleasant but firm way, "Too loud Danny, and we have a guest!"

"Who cares?"

She shrugs easily and explains, "My little brother. He's fourteen."

"Oh, I have a fourteen-year-old sister," I grin. "Maybe we can set them up on a date."

Amused, Cynthia shakes her head. "Somehow I don't think your sister would like that."

"Surprise, she doesn't like anything."

"Wonderful, a match made in hell." She stops to contemplate. "Tell you what, let's go for a walk. Do you mind?"

Hey, there's not much I'm not going to do for her! "Fantastic," I concur. "Can I use your phone for sex? I mean, for a sec?" My face turns brutally red due to my Freudian slip.

She pretends not to notice my stupid faux pas. "Absolutely, it's right there in the kitchen. After you're finished could you stroll down the hall and chat with Danny? Just consider it the biggest challenge of your lifetime. I have to go upstairs and change."

"Not a problem." I try not to show how eager I am to please her.

Once I enter the kitchen it hits me that all the walls I've seen in this huge house are painted snow white. Everything is incredibly clean and orderly. I ring up Mom and let her in on my whereabouts and plans. Even though she tells me that's okay, "but don't be late for dinner," there's something in her voice telling me it isn't. Typical.

I follow strange screeching sounds from the TV down the hallway. The family room, untidy compared to the rest of the house, brings me a glimpse of Danny's shadowed profile. He's on the slim side, not actually skinny, but lean. Up high, beside a fireplace, window curtains are drawn and the lights are off. Although he's aware that I'm in the room with him, those images on the screen are magnets for his eyes. He's extended his slouch the full length of the sofa. He's watching pro wrestling. This gives me two good reasons to remain on my feet.

"How are you, Danny? I'm Jim." That's me, forever friendly.

At first I don't think he's going to say a word. "Awesome," he slowly drawls out with no eye contact. "Ya like wrestlin'?" I'm amazed he can squeeze out a three-word phrase in this catatonic state of his. He has the usual high school junior's baby-face.

Finally I answer him, "No, I'm into soccer."

"Soccer sucks," he sneers. He reconvenes staring into the TV.

"Wrestling's fake," I report.

There is a pause. "S'awesome," he concludes, switching me off.

I observe the program he's so immersed in to try to understand its appeal. Two steroid-laden wrestlers are standing in the centre of the ring, trash-talking each other. Soon they are focused on a fanatical, incessant ritual involving punching and the smashing of chairs. Other wrestlers 'spontaneously' rush out from a gigantic entrance ramp in tune to carefully scripted music, bright coloured lights, and frenzied fan reaction that is all mixed together. In no time there are about twelve different 300-pound bodies in the small ring. It's ridiculous and I have not seen one wrestling move. There is, however, plenty of bad acting.

Cynthia's reappearance is a relief, as she walks up to the TV and turns down the sound. I sure am in awe of the way she takes control of every situation that I have so far witnessed. "Danny? Jim and I are going out for a walk. Want to come?"

"No," he answers flatly, "and get out of the way, will ya!"

"Have it your way. See you later, little bro."

Before we can open the front door to freedom he shouts back, "I'm not little and call me Dan, not Danny!"

Cynthia rolls her eyes and grins at me as we both hear the TV volume turned up again. "Okay, big Dan."

"That's better!"

I'VE LEFT MY BACKPACK IN HER KITCHEN and will pick it up after our walk. We're outdoors. Dressed in a sky blue T-shirt and jeans, she asks, "You want to see the Falls?"

My own clothes are pretty ordinary: white casual short-sleeve shirt and light brown khakis, cut-off at the knees. "I'm game." My mouth turns desert dry.

This is so great! We're about to embark on a three-mile hike! I'm going to see the original Fissure Rock site. More important, I will be alone with Cynthia Sacalla, except we'll be walking along a busy roadside.

"This way," and with her head she motions a direction opposite to the one I was expecting.
"But I thought the highway was—"
"Short cut. Less than a mile through the woods."
I say what I think, "Oh," and give her my biggest smile yet.

OUR JOURNEY BEGINS in an alleyway behind the main street stores, where garbage is piled for pick-up. The smell is gross. We both ignore it and find ourselves at the beginning of a path leading into the woods out of town. As we enter, I realize this is the first time I've had a chance to do any exploring around here. Concentrating on school, dealing with my family and the new house has been my whole life for the week. I'm glad Cynthia is helping me let loose a bit. Now the sweet smell of healthy trees, with their dwelling songbirds, fills my nose and ears. I can't keep my eyes off her. It's agony!

Along the dirt path, tree roots stick out above the surface and we have to be on the lookout not to trip over them. The same goes for tops of rocks, which pop up almost like icebergs in a swirling sea. Twists and turns en route cause me to glance back, occasionally, and all I see are blankets of trees behind us—a dark green shroud. No town noises, no motors from the close-by highway, can be detected.

"You're a quiet guy," she suddenly says.

We both stop.

I look at her face. Sun patches flicker through spaces between branches of thick leaves. My forced smile meets her beautiful image. Her body seems to waver in the glowing dancing sunlight. "We don't have this kind of scenery in the city."

Here we are, deep in the woods. I want to reach out and grab her, have her! I'm disgusted by these primitive urges surging through me. To go farther where she leads me, yes, and in the same breath I . . . I'm lost. I'm very lost.

"Ah," Cynthia sighs playfully, her voice chiming up an octave.

"The urban urchin is mesmerized by our rural vistas. He's come up here in hopes of reforming his evil metropolitan ways, and it's working like a charm. Am I right?" She's light-hearted, so naturally at ease, and so articulate!

With pretend relief I mumble, "I guess." Then I start to laugh. Several seconds pass. I can't stop. You know that crazy machine-gun type laugh that hurts your stomach muscles? That's what's happening and I'm gasping for air. Tense, tears forming, flowing from my eyes, this whole scene is too unreal.

Cynthia studies me while I cry like some pathetic town drunk.

"Sorry," I say. At some point I regain control of myself and feel dumb. This spur of madness washed out of me, I bring my hands up to my face to wipe away these unexplainable salty liquid secretions.

Tenderly my companion blocks my hands with her wrists and dries my wet face with her soft fingers. She hugs me warm and close.

Trembling, I hold onto her like she's my mother.

"Everything's all right," she whispers. "I understand you, Jim."

What do I say to this? "Well," I speak through a sore raspy throat, "I don't know why I was just bawling like a baby." Fiercely I shake my head and scowl in disbelief.

"Don't you see? Your entire life has changed in, what has it been, seven days?" Her beautiful blue eyes beam into my green ones as she releases her hold on me and takes a step back. For some reason I'm unable to answer, so she continues, "You put on such a brave face at school. How do you keep that act together all the time?"

Wow, I thought I was pretty good at being wise beyond my years. I admit it, she's got me beat. The thing is her superior insights don't bother me. "You've made me feel better already." I sound so sheepish!

Cynthia puts her hands on my upper arms. "My mom says we all need a shoulder to cry on from time to time." Again she lets me go and resumes walking. "Come on."

Hollow, I follow.

WHERE THIS PATH ENDS, trees disappear and a rough opening of long grass and different sized boulders floods with light from a cloudless sky. Sounds of running water transform me into an excited child. I dash past her and out into the new space. This tiny expanse stops with a cliff. About 30 feet down a dwarf lake sparkles. Standing on the edge I view two waterfalls on the other extreme. It's a majestic Lilliputian sight. Water splashes musically.

Forgotten is my emotional outburst in the forest. "Am I dreaming?" I shout, listening to the echo of my voice and laughing with more self-control than before. I have no desire to lose it again.

"Enjoy," Cynthia invites, sitting on a big rock and smiling knowingly. "After you've lived here a while you get used to it all."

Putting my hands on my hips I inhale deeply, absorbing the wall of trees and rock surrounding the lake with its twin falls. I'm imagining myself as that earliest European settler, finding this place for the first time. I fix my eyes on the lake: each ripple, every sunlit reflected shimmer. "Why would they ever move the town from this spot?"

"Don't know." Cynthia's on her feet again. "Let me take you down to the dock we built last summer."

WE'RE SITTING BESIDE EACH OTHER on the sturdy wooden dock. She has her jeans rolled up to her knees, as we dangle our feet into the lake. I am in some warm heaven. Out of the blue she asks me, "So you hang around with Andy?"

She's clutched my curiosity. "Not really. We have lunch together. I don't know many other people around—"

"Sorry about that," Cynthia interjects. "Lunch hour is one of the few times I get to meet with my student council. We have to plan a whole array of things."

"It's fine," I say. "I kind of figured that." Venturing further I ask, "Do you like Andy?"

Her pause is noted. "Oh, Andy's a sweet guy. He just doesn't . . . join in. I think it's great you have lunch with him. But you don't want to do more than that. I mean charity has its limits, right?"

I'm completely confused, so I remain silent.

She reaches out with her right foot and coils it around my left calf. "Has Andy ever said anything to you about me?"

I look at her in guarded shock. "No." Swallowing hard, I stare down into the water at our shaky mirror images. I've just lied to her, and I wonder if there's any chance she does not know this. "Why?"

Cynthia kisses me on the cheek. "Not important." She has her arm around my waist and slides her foot up and down the lower part of my leg, bare skin against bare skin. "You have nice legs, Jim. Lean, smooth, strong."

What to do, what to do? Everything's happening faster than my imagination can keep up with. Returning the favour, I put my arm around her waist and make a bold response even as my voice shakes, "Not as smooth as yours."

She giggles, "And you're a smooth talker, too."

Our lips touch. Nothing else happens, but it's still amazing! We sit there forever. Clouds float in. The sun turns red and slowly bleeds itself out of the sky.

The walk back to town is a silent mystical one.

ROCK FOUR

HOW CAN I TALK about the rest of my weekend? All else pales in comparison to Friday afternoon when Cynthia kissed me, hugged me, wrapped her leg around mine. Yes, my first kiss. I've never been so close to a girl, and boy did it feel great! Nothing Dad, Mom or even Lisa can say or do is capable of shaking the spell I'm under—my time spent with Cynthia. Am I feeling love or lust? I've already made up my mind to tell no one, certainly not Andy.

Here I sit in our living room on a Sunday evening, with my parents and my sister, watching some lame sitcom on TV. During numerous commercial breaks my parents, thinking they are being tactful, bombard me using an assortment of cumbersome questions.

Mom starts the show while the toothpaste advertisement brushes away. "Parent-teacher-student interviews begin in a few weeks. Are you getting ready?"

I'm thinking about Cynthia.

"Jim?" she asks, nearly startling me.

"Sure. Everything is all right."

Dad does commentary, "They never did that back in the city, did they? I think it's a fantastic idea to have the students there also. Doing it so early in the school year helps you get off on the right foot. Don't you agree, son?"

"Uh-huh." I figure it's my duty as a teenager not to tell them too much. After all, what is there to tell? I don't want to stop thinking about Cynthia.

Lisa inadvertently helps me. The program has reappeared and she spouts out, "If the only thing we can to do in this useless town is watch TV, at least you could keep quiet when it's on!"

EVERYTHING CHANGED FOR ME at the Falls, yet nothing did. Example: My second week at FRH has begun and every day Cynthia waves her hand and shows off her teeth to me from the opposite end of the cafeteria, where she continues sitting with her student council cronies. In English class, since Mr. King is strict about seating arrangements, she's on the other side of the room. But can't she find some time to talk to me after school, at least? She hasn't spoken one word to me. I thought we'd planted the seed of a real relationship. There was a tender closeness, that heart-to-heart chat. All for nothing? This is like re-living my barren first week all over again.

Maybe I'm expected to make the next move, to seize the initiative? I can roll with punches easily, but being in charge is not my thing. Oh, I could lead Bryan, Mason and Wendy when I lived in the city . . . up here is different. I'm basically a foreigner, not yet trusted by the locals and vice-versa. I have to walk a careful line. Sorry to say I have this feeling I've been a little rude to my pal, Andy, who drones on and on each lunch hour about his favourite baseball team, like I care! I hate baseball; it's boring. Don't ask me what my exact words are. I don't do too well remembering conversations verbatim. My attention is not focused on what I say to him. Do I sound a tad pissed? It's only because I'm thinking about Cynthia.

ANOTHER EVENING. I'm sitting in my bedroom scratching a few phrases at my desk. Before I know it, my guitar is on my lap and I'm arranging power chords. It doesn't take long when I write a song, probably because my attention span is short. I daydream a lot. Actually that's an understatement. In less than twenty minutes I emerge on stage to sing my newest composition to an adoring audience.

Too fast, this current tide
Cruise into a canoe glide
And touch the water's grace
And feel you're in just the right place

Download the brains of man
Still love is all I understand
Black canopy's revolving stars
Wisk away these smoke-filled cars

Whenever I hold you near
I'm a romantic pioneer
Cold in the snow
Riding reindeer

Computer-hard software
No time to stop and stare
Only gold-stemmed roses grow
Which is a fact as most of us know

Whenever I hold you near
I'm a romantic pioneer
Cold in the snow
Riding reindeer

 The applause is deafening. I take a bow, wave to the crowd, and feel like a fool as usual. Silly little pipe dream.
 And again, I'm thinking about Cynthia.

ROCK FIVE

UNEVENTFUL WEEKS GO BY. Then that unavoidable Thursday night arrives. Dad, as usual, must work late at Sacalla Real Estate. I have no choice but to go alone with Mom to the parent-teacher-student interviews. It's supposed to be set up so you and your parents meet with each teacher for five minutes. Since I'm new at the school, we are to consult with the Guidance Counsellor for about fifteen minutes—no teachers.

While we sit and wait in the office on hard wooden chairs, I overhear a conversation between Mr. King and another man from a classroom through the wall. My English teacher's voice is pleasant and professional, "Mr. Pitt, I believe Todd needs a tutor . . ."

The other man is definitely angry. "Coz ya can't teach him right, that's why!"

Listening to his father, I can sort of understand why Todd is such a total loser. Everyone at school knows his dad drinks, smokes, swears heavily. Mr. Pitt also likes to use his fists when he runs out of words. They say the apple doesn't fall far from the tree. Todd's the kind of bulky aggressive kid who I make a key point of avoiding. Like a lot of students here, he lives on a farm outside the town and is bussed in everyday.

"I've tried helping Todd compose a simple sentence, but he doesn't seem to care."

Todd's dad rages on, "Yeah, can't say as I blame him! He tells me you're always pickin' on him all the time!"

I see that my mother is nervous listening to this (nothing out of the ordinary there). 'Nervous' is her middle name.

Meanwhile my teacher is good at keeping his cool. "Sir, that is not true . . ."

"Now you're sayin' me and my boy, we're both liars! What's your name again?"

"Mr. King."

"Whatever! You only bin here a year and ya got some learnin' to do 'bout how things work in this town!"

"Mr. Pitt, I am trying to find a way to help your son . . ."

"All you gotta do is give him passing marks and get off his back! You gotta wife?"

My teacher's words indicate he's baffled by this out-of-left-field question. "Pardon me? No, I'm single . . ."

"You gotta be 'bout forty. What's wrong with ya?"

This is getting intriguing as I try to listen for more. I think we're all addicted to gossip, never mind how hard we deny it.

Todd says, "Dad, let's get the hell outta here?"

"Shut your goddamn hole!" Mr. Pitt hollers.

Finally Mom and I are ushered into a tiny sub-office by the secretary, and I'm kind of let down at not being able to hear more from the voices through the office wall. On the other hand they've shaken me, affected me in ways I can't explain.

Mom and I sit down in the new location while a strange skinny woman starts her onslaught. "Jim, are you happy at this school?" Her voice is one lazy monotone, like the dull blade of a butter knife scrapping away at burnt toast.

A smidgen off-balance I mutter, "Uh, yeah, it's okay." What is this?

"Your teachers have told me that you drift off during class, your homework is seldom done—"

"Hey, I'm quiet. I don't disturb the class." My feathers are ruffled.

She gives me an idiotic look, which suits her by the way, and with her beady little eyes she scans my mom who naturally says nothing. The black-haired woman rattles on, "Well, that's true enough. They would like you to speak out more . . . to participate in class . . . to show you're comprehending—"

I interrupt a second time, "Well I'm really new here. We moved the day before school started and it was a four-hour drive, and the city is a lot different from this insignificant town of yours!" (Best defence is a good offence.)

"Jim!" This time Mom's shocked, though that's all she can think of to say.

I can't believe how irritated I'm getting . . . please don't tell me I'm turning into another Lisa. Swiftly reviewing the flight path I've taken, I opt to make adjustments and alter my course. "Look, I'm a nice guy. Honest." I manoeuvre my eyes and smile in a puppy dog kind of way.

The woman doesn't buy it. Still I am granted some slack on my leash. "There's no need to panic, Jim. We do know that you're new. We've been in touch with your former school. Yesterday your transcripts arrived."

"It's kind of hard to get any work done in a big city school, with nearly 40 kids in every class!" Feeling my lips shaping into a frown, I'm staring ferociously at her.

Mom gets involved. "Jim, you will let Mrs. Arseneault finish."

So that's what her name is. If my mother is taking sides with this black-haired twit, I'm definitely going to lose my temper. Then again I can't blame Mom. She doesn't know anything about these bureaucratic boneheads.

"Thank you, Mrs. Bridgeman," she states in her sickening business-like fashion. "Jim, the documents reveal your obvious high-level intelligence. Despite this, your marks were barely above 50, except English in which you did exceptionally well. Your former teachers commented that you have potential, but you seldom finish what you start. They, too, noted that you were easily distracted—"

My hands slap down hard on my knees, causing both women to take special note of me. "Where is Dad?" I sternly ask my mother, giving her my mixed expression of rage and fear.

"Darling, you know he's working late."

"Yes!" I exclaim. "But I think he should be here! If I'm doing this bad—"

The new woman attempts to put me at ease. "Jim, we want to help you. Please relax." She's not fooling me; her intonation is cold and insincere.

Slowly bobbing my head up and down, my eyes study her

way-too-shiny floor. Tilting my head up at the ugly fluorescent light, I see and hear a big buzzing fly. It zips around the room as Mrs. Aerosol continues to spray the pressure on me.

"Have you made any friends since you've been with us?" She waits.

Taking my mind off the fly I reply, "Yes. Andy Bradford."

Mom puts in her shaky two cents worth again. "Oh yes, Jim has mentioned Andy. We hear he's a big baseball fan. He sounds very nice." I do a roll with my eyes, which thankfully neither woman catches. My mom spends most of her life in la-la land, where everything and everyone is simply 'nice' or 'not nice.'

Then I pitch in with gusto, "And Cynthia Sacalla!" I grin sly as a fox, clever name-dropper that I am.

"Ah yes, Cynthia," the woman sings cheerfully under her breath. "She's on the honour roll."

Mom's pretty face is puzzled. "The girl you went for a walk with that first Friday, after school?"

I say nothing. I'm waiting for my newest adversary to react to all this.

She begins by totally downplaying my association with Cynthia. "Well, it was certainly generous of her to take time off from her busy schedule to show you some of the sites."

Sarcastically I'm thinking, 'Oh no, Cynthia would never do such a thing as a result of her liking me a whole lot, would she, you brainless wonder?' This Aerosol woman is really something else!

And she's not done yet. "As a matter of fact you might want to regard her as a peer model. Cynthia Sacalla is the most professional type student we've ever had at FRH. She is fulfilling her potential."

Silence, except that damn fly just keeps buzzing at me. Aerosol's penetrating eyes are signalling . . . what? A cue for me to say something? Why do people constantly expect me to read from a script that I don't have? I finally ask, "Is this over, now?"

Mom gives me a mild reprimand. "A little impolite, don't you think, dear?"

Mrs. Aerosol shuffles through papers in a thick folder, and seems to have found the page she was looking for. "Andy Bradford," she reads out the name of my other friend, checking out his record like she's a police officer or something. "I thought as much. He also made the honour roll. Last year," she adds. Then, "How do you feel about him leaving?"

I violently swipe at the fly as it rushes by. "What do you mean, leaving?"

AN HOUR LAPSES between the time we get back home from the school interview and Dad's return from work. He looks worn out. Mom fills him in on all the gory details. My father rarely disappoints me. I am given a pep talk about the importance of a good education and how I must strive hard to concentrate and get my studying done on time. I love my dad, and Mom is plainly satisfied with his fatherly work on me tonight, especially considering he's put in another 14-hour day.

I climb the stairs to my room, close the door, disrobe down to my boxers and fall asleep under my warm quilt. Almost immediately a bad dream painfully pulls me inside it. An unwelcome blast from the past returns to me, a real incident from my life as an eight-year-old . . .

"Fight all you want . . . I got ya!" Laughter from above, a so-called friend straddled on my chest in his backyard.

Me struggling, "Get off me! Not fair. You tripped me!"

He grabs my wrists and pins them to the ground while staring into my defeated eyes with glee, "Everything's fair . . . long as I win."

I try, impossibly, to squirm away from him. "I mean it, get off me!"

A big triumphant smile covers his face. "You're not goin' nowhere . . . not till I say so." He taps first one side of my face with my own trapped hand, and when I turn my head, he taps the other side using my other trapped hand.

"Stop it! Come on, let me go!" Panic prickles through me.
"Ah, are you gonna cry now? Let's see some tears, little baby." Laughter.
I'm angry. *"You just wait! When I get up—"*
He continues to taunt, *"Oh, I'm so scared. You're my prisoner. Too bad, huh? For you, that is!"*
Even though it's hopeless, I'm kicking about, trying to break free. *"You asshole!"*
"Oh, you swore!" He squeezes my nose with his fingers. *"This is your punishment. Okay, say somethin' else."*
"Stop it, stop it! I mean it. I'm serious."
He laughs heartily. *"You sound so funny."* He releases my nose. In his eyes, a dreadful glare gives hints of new ideas forming behind them.
I'll never recover from this humiliation. Trapped . . . laughed at . . . more . . .
"Hey," he says in a strained and excited voice, *"I bet I can do whatever I want to ya!"*
My eyes open wide in desperate fear.

I force myself back to consciousness, sitting up in bed and breathing fast. This cold sweating body reminds me that I can never escape from my own history, no matter what. Try as hard as I do to forget, it always has a habit of catching up with me. But I think there are plenty of people like me. I sure hope I'm not the only one.

NEXT DAY, approaching our regular lunch table in the school cafeteria, I look down at Andy, waiting for an acknowledgment that I'm there. Instead he examines the sandwich in his hand.

Clearing my throat I greet him, "Hey."

Andy sits there, frowning. "Can't find another table?" He's royally pissed off.

I scrunch up my face into a question mark.

At this he finally turns his gaze on me. "You're acting like you're clueless."

"Only cuz I am."

"Oh, man! How about when you told me I could shove my baseball up my ass?"

"What?" That's not like me. Did I say such a thing? Is Andy playing a little joke? I mean there was that warning about Cynthia and he was wrong about her.

"And that's just the beginning," he steams ahead. "All week you've been trashing me to my face and I really don't need it, okay?"

Andy pauses for my reaction. I'm in too much disbelief to give him one.

"Jim? You're not going to say you don't remember saying those things, are you? Just like you didn't listen when I said 'knock it off' or 'that's enough'?"

Damn. I think he's right. Now that he's repeating all this, it is sounding vaguely familiar . . . like a bad dream. I've never seen Andy in such a rotten mood.

"So why not find yourself another table, huh?"

Before I can stop myself, my voice breaks, "Andy, I'm really sorry, man."

He's not sold on my sincerity. "Yeah? Took you a long time."

I realize I have to explain. "Sometimes I get so preoccupied with other stuff, you know, and I don't pay any attention to what I say. I never mean to hurt anybody, honest." I stand still, wondering. Seconds slowly tick off in my head.

"All right," he sighs, "sit down if you want."

I promise myself from this point on to start my brain before using my voice box. I've settled into my normal seat facing him. "Andy, I consider you a friend."

"Same here," he responds grudgingly. Yup, he's still hurting. Poor guy. My fault.

I ask outright, "Is this why you're leaving?"

"Who told you?"

"That guidance counsellor woman. Last night."

"Mrs. Arseneault?"

"Yeah, her."

"No, Jim, I'm not leaving because of you." The insulted edge in his tone remains. "Are you happy now?"

"Of course not," I tell him emphatically. "We're buds. What's with this?"

"We're moving to the city."

Privately I'm thinking, 'After Andy's gone, who am I going to have lunch with?' Publicly I ask him, "But why?"

"My father's relocating his law office down there. Bigger market, more money. Probably better for me in a lot of ways, too. Since it's not for another couple of weeks, I thought I'd tell you later on. Drawn-out good-byes suck anyway."

I'm looking across the large room where Cynthia has just left with her student council trailing behind her. I suppose she's off to one of her many meetings in the name of the school. Then I remind myself where I am and the conversation I'm having. "Andy, I still don't get it."

"Yeah, I know," he says sad-faced, having noticed that Cynthia's exit distracted me for a second. "But you'll understand later. Your day will come."

ROCK SIX

THE REST OF THAT FRIDAY AFTERNOON hits me even worse. I'm walking slowly behind Fissure Rock High along the football field and it's starting to rain . . . spitting, spraying. An enormous canvas cloud covers the sky and doesn't move, just darkens the day. I've noticed these trees in north-country change colour early. Other kids are to my left, right, in front and behind me, also on their way home. They ignore me, of course. Almost all are in pairs or groups. Friends. I feel alone.

Cynthia? Too busy, that's all. Looks like Arseneault was correct. She'd merely been pointing out a local attraction to me as a goodwill gesture for 'the new kid,' an act of charity. I shudder at the thought of that as a possibility. The fact remains: we were at the Falls alone. She kissed me, hugged me, and a wee bit more. Does this match the definition of a guided tour, even if it was casual? I feel confused.

I've got to remember a couple of crucial things. First, Andy will be gone from here in two weeks. Second, I must pay closer attention to my schoolwork. Since Arseneault's assault, I know both Mom and Dad will be on constant watch around me, smiling when they see me crack open a book to read or when I take notes, frowning if I don't. That's their subtle way. I feel pressure.

Mom was wise to buy me this waterproof knapsack because the old H20 is now pouring down hard. I'm thinking of springtime, when it rains like this, when hundreds of worms wiggle out of the ground to get some air to breathe—on top of the grass, the gravel running track, and on asphalt pathways. Lots of them probably get squashed underneath shoes and boots, others likely lay drowned in small puddles, and some might survive to go back down when it's dry enough. We're studying Hamlet in Mr. King's English class. I've already read it a couple of times on my own and I've seen some movie versions. At one point Hamlet says, "A man may fish with the worm that hath eat of a king and eat of the fish that hath fed of that worm." I don't go fishing and I don't eat fish, but I know I can't escape death. Someday the worms will get me. I feel sad.

Then I look around me at the shapes of humans my own age. I see and hear them laughing, talking. They're young and healthy. Their whole lives are ahead of them. Seems like forever. But it's not. While they cover themselves as best they can to ward off the rain, I can see the ultimate futility of their efforts. It will end for all of us and when it does, most likely that will be it for all time. Eternal nothingness. My stomach churns a bit at the bleak prospect. Oh well, at least we won't exist any longer to know the difference, so big deal. Right? But what if there is some kind of consciousness that continues on forever? Never ending. Some other dimension? Hamlet fears this in his famous "To be or not to be" soliloquy: "But that the dread of something after death, the undiscovered country from whose bourn no traveller returns, puzzles the will and makes us rather bear those ills we have than fly to others that we know not of . . . ."

It makes no sense to dwell further on it, so I don't. Everyday is a new life. Might as well hang in there, because who knows what could happen today, tomorrow, next year, whenever. And there are so many things to see and do. Yep, hang onto your life as long as you can, that's my motto. Even as I tell all this to myself, I notice the hands inside my pockets are wet with worry.

BY THE TIME I MAKE IT to the house, I figure my rain-drenched mood should lift. I hang up my dripping jacket and knapsack in the hall closet.

Mom's red-rimmed eyes snail to where I stand. There's no sense in asking what's wrong because she'll never tell me. That's her. Lisa's home, the squeal of heavy metal music coming from her room is a dead give-away. Too bad she isn't into one of those synthetic boy bands; they're easier on the eardrums. Clearly she and Mom have had another of their clashes.

My mother looks at me, and our green eyes share a stare. "How was your day, darling?" She shows a smile of sorrow.

"All right," I lie. "What's happening here?"

"Nothing much," she answers, not telling the truth either. She takes cover in the kitchen to prepare dinner. "Your father has to work late tonight."

Looking at her back I say, "This is Friday."

"I know."

BOUNDING UP THE STAIRS, I'm about to do something I normally don't: pay Lisa a visit. No doubt my sister is somehow responsible for Mom's sadness.

Reaching the upper level hallway, I walk towards the screeches and shrieks of her favourite music. I knock and without waiting for the permission I know I won't get, I open her door.

From above the horrific noise she manages to shout, "Out!"

Hmm, she's been busy at the computer terminal on an internet chat line, and now she quickly terminates her connection.

Closing the door behind me, I plug my ears with my two index fingers and smile like Goofy in direct contrast to her sullen expression. This is a signal for her to turn down the noise and talk to me or else I'll stand here for . . . eternity? Worse, I'll tell Mom about her using a chat room, causing her to be permanently disconnected from the net. She might even fear I'll spill the beans about Gerald and her, although I would never really do that.

Something works. Lisa actually shuts down her stereo machinery to take me on. "What?" She sits on her bed, angry, a wildcat ready to pounce.

Seeing her like this, a more creative strategy seeps into my mind. In a soft voice I ask, "Hey, Lisa? Do you think we'll ever get Sideline back?"

For a few seconds I've succeeded. She gives me the strangest, most surprised gape I've seen on her in a long while. As with most unexpected things from Lisa, this doesn't last long. She returns to being bitchy. "Stupid question. Here's an easy answer: No!"

"Come on," I continue in my nice big brotherly way, "don't you miss him?"

"Who, Dad?" She gives me a quick serious look. Interesting.

"No, Sideline." I'm just as serious.

"That dumb cat?"

Weird. Now I can't recall if she ever liked Sideline or not. I assumed she did . . . ?

Lisa throws a mouthful of sharp tacks at me: "This is you all over, Jimmy! Grow up, will you? Dad's never home and you're worried about Sideline—"

"Whoa, hold it," I stop her. "I want to know why Mom's been crying."

She laughs briefly. It's derisive laughter; I would expect nothing else from her. "Let's just say she and you are definitely mother and son, get it?"

My left eye squints at her as I turn my head in the same direction. "Meaning what?"

Lisa marches to her door and swings it open with authority. "You both need a good dose of reality. Now get out!"

I leisurely stroll toward the exit, and put on my nonchalant mask again, the one she hates with a passion. "Well Leese, I can't stick around here gabbing with you all afternoon. I've got important things to do. See ya." And I'm gone, my sister slamming the door behind me.

Because I enjoy bugging the hell out of her with my customary humour, perhaps I have a spoonful of sadistic tendency in me.

ROCK SEVEN

DAD'S WORKING OVERTIME; we have a quiet dinner. Mom and I comfort each other that, sooner or later, his workload will decrease and we'll see more of Bill Bridgeman at home. Lisa scoffs at this notion. She doesn't actually say anything, just shapes a sardonic smile and gives out a ridiculing snort. If I was a psychiatrist, I'd think her hostility is like a defensive shield helping her feel on top of things she can't control. I wonder if she'll ever be able to find some kind of happiness in her life. I'm no dummy, things aren't going too great for our family at present and I'm also feeling down about it, but there's always hope in me that things might turn out better. I'm trying my best to improve matters myself by not reacting to Lisa's nonsense. It's a start.

I help Mom with the dishes, figuring I should since Lisa left the table before we'd finished eating.

The phone rings. Will it be Dad saying he's on his way, or that he'll be delayed even longer than expected?

Mom answers, hesitates. "Just a moment, please," and holds the phone out to me.

Figuring it's Andy, I wipe my hands dry before I take the phone from her. "Hello?"

"Hi. What are you up to tonight?"

Following my split-second jumble of confusion, I brighten up. "Cynthia! How are you?" Did I give her my phone number? No, she must have gone to the trouble of finding it out.

"If you're not doing anything, why not come over? I have to stay home with Danny."

"Great!" I reply.

Her voice is in a sing-song mode. "Any time you're ready."

"I'll leave in fifteen minutes." I hang up the phone and smile, sensing no one else is on the planet with Cynthia and me. Life just got a whole lot better.

THOSE FIFTEEN MINUTES are put to good use. I check my reflection in the bathroom mirror. I've overheard girls at school whisper to each other that they think I'm cute. I'd rather be seen as ruggedly handsome, thanks very much, but I guess for now I'll have to live with being cute. I'm glad I have no signs of acne. Undressing, I wonder when I'm going to start growing more hair on my legs, arms, chest and face. It's embarrassing in Gym class because I have only a bit sprouting on my shins, and my underarms are furry enough, except everywhere else is smooth or peach-fuzz at best. At least I'm well toned—not too thin or fat. Finally I step into the shower to wash away my stupid thoughts. Like Superman emerging from Clark Kent, in no time I'm into a freshly pressed pair of cords and a multi-coloured brand-name sweater. Next I do the hair brushing, toothpaste and mouthwash thing. I feel potent . . . could be I overdid it using Dad's cologne.

Stepping outside, I see the day surrendering to growing darkness. Rain puddles have shrunken. Early October weather sometimes teases us mortals with a tiny taste of fall, followed by brief reminders of summer. It's so unfortunate that I don't know Mrs. Arseneault's home phone number. 'Guess what, Mrs. A? I've been invited to Cynthia Sacalla's house . . . yeah, that's right. She's found time in her busy schedule and she'll be spending that time with me . . . again! It might be an all-nighter, Mrs. A! What do you say? Ha!' It'd be an understatement to say I'm alive with confidence. The walk from my house to Cynthia's is exactly twelve minutes . . . I'm wearing my reliable wristwatch with a second hand . . . nothing digital about me.

As I turn onto the street and face the front of her house at the very end, I don't mind saying I feel nervous. So many butterflies are flapping around in my stomach, I have to stop for a moment to get them slowed down. Running through my mind, like mice on tiny treadmills, are all the things that could possibly go wrong.

I hope I don't screw this up. Don't let me say one word that would kill me dead with her! I'm a big King Lear fan, and once more Shakespeare saves my sorry ass as I recall this line, "O, that way madness lies; let me shun that! No more of that." So I shake off the negativity and uncertainty, and boldly march down the sidewalk towards her house like a conqueror about to be!

DAN OPENS THE DOOR shortly after I ring the bell. His curly brown head comes up to the bridge of my nose, and he's way more enthusiastic than during our first encounter. "Hey, come on through! She's on the can." (Definitely too much information.)

I follow this newly energized kid into their spacious family room, and am surprised to see the TV set is off. "Do you have any brothers, other sisters? Parents?" The only people I've seen in this house so far are Cynthia and him.

He squints and studies me up and down. "Just Mom. Want a beer?"

The last three words grab my attention the most. "No thanks," I slowly answer.

Dan shrugs, "Suit yourself. Sit down somewhere if you want. Be right back." Then he strides out of the room. He's being very friendly and seems thrilled that I'm here.

Suspicious at the best of times, I find a chair facing away from the television which gives me a vantage point over anybody who enters the room. It's the same setting, well-lit this time, an interior decorator's dream. Features I didn't notice on my first visit catch my attention. A bit cluttered (clearly this is where Dan spends much of his time), there are carefully arranged bookshelves, oil paintings on the walls, two sofas, a few chairs and of course that old-fashioned fireplace in the far corner with a window above and to the side. Two white walls face each other, while the other two are wood paneled. Yeah, 'carefully arranged' best describes the entire house.

When Dan returns, he stands at the centre of the room on the large Persian carpet and takes huge gulps from the bottle in his hand. I can't say I'm not surprised watching a 14-year-old drinking beer, but I've seen stranger things. He clearly enjoys feeling like a man. It's written all over his face and it keeps examining mine. Well, I figure, let him enjoy his buzz.

"So," I break the ice, "where's your mom?"

Settling into one of the sofas, Dan stretches out and laughs. "Aw," he replies with carefree haughtiness, "who knows? She comes home. Usually in early morning, if you know what I mean." Dan's an experienced drinker. After every fragmented sentence, he takes a swig of beer. "Sometimes see 'er before school. Maybe breakfast together. Here on Saturday. And Sunday. Afternoons. About it." He burps. Wow, he's trying so hard to be macho it's like screaming out of his pores.

"Is Cynthia here?" I finally wonder aloud.

Dan downs the rest and places the empty bottle on an end table. Then he shouts, "Hey! Your new boyfriend's here!"

"Hi, Jim," I hear her welcoming voice from way upstairs. "Try to put up with my brother for five more minutes . . . important phone call."

Suddenly, Dan jumps to his feet and is standing at the centre of the carpet. "Come over here," he demands.

"What?" This kid's got me dumbfounded.

"Stand up!" he orders, speaking with an urgency that unnerves me. "I wanna show you somethin'."

I cautiously get to my feet, thinking there's something about that look in his eyes (like when Sideline sees a mouse). My worst fears are realized.

As soon as I'm standing, he darts behind me and I'm locked in his Full Nelson. "Let's see ya get out of this hold, soccer boy!" He laughs in a maniacal manner.

"Dan, what's this? Let go." I'm waving with both arms, but mine is a useless effort.

He's got the hold on very tight and is naturally not going to release it on my command. "Ya think wrestlin's fake, eh? 'Can you handle this?'" He has all those clichéd phrases from the TV rasslin' shows working for him, that's for sure.

I don't much like playing puppet boy for some midget minor niner! I begin to lean forward, knowing he's lighter than me and I can easily flip him right over, thus breaking the hold.

"No, you don't!" he shouts. Before I can raise him off his feet, he kicks mine from under me. I plop down on my butt, and he lands on his knees behind me, maintaining the Full Nelson hold all the while. "Now, let's see ya get away!"

The next few minutes take way too long to pass by. I decide not to struggle anymore. Why show him what I know to be the truth? I'm stuck, his prisoner even. I've learned from years before . . . the only way for me to retain some particle of dignity is to pretend I don't care enough to even try to escape. "You're really good, Dan." I throw in a forced chuckle, restrained though I am. "You gonna to turn pro, someday?"

Just when I think I can't be any more embarrassed, Cynthia walks in. She smiles at her brother.

Right away he lets me go and sits down on the sofa again, a big satisfied grin carved onto his face. Dan turns on the TV.

Still stunned, I remain seated on the carpet.

Cynthia speaks, "Sorry, Jim. I forgot to warn you about Danny's wrestling-crazed mind."

"Name's Dan!" he screams out.

Feeling a lot more than ridiculous I stand up and smile. "No problem." Except it is a problem. The familiar defeated ache in my fragile pride returns. Moving up here was supposed to erase that awful memory from my past, and now I just got out-wrestled by this no-good kid! It hurts so much inside that I nearly start punching away at my own face for being such a worthless piece of crap! I can sense the whole world laughing loudly at me. Again.

In her cheerful way Cynthia says, "Let's go up to my room."

Hesitating, I'm amazed at how swiftly my moods can swing. "Lead the way," I grin like the cunning stud I wish I could be.

Dan laughs the way a typical brat his age always does. "Keep it quiet up there, so I can concentrate on my TV watchin'!" He's kind of like the male version of Lisa.

Cynthia points to the evidence of the beer bottle. "Dan, you better sit tight and not one more trip to the fridge for another beer. I'll be keeping my door open and you know how good my ears are."

She'll make a great mother. Her tone is forceful and businesslike, yet I haven't once seen her drop the special charm. Cynthia has this aura about her that goes beyond mere beauty. Nothing can rattle her. She's one of those rare people keeping all situations under control. Just being around her is a breath of fresh air.

HER ROOM is not exactly what I expected. Sure her bed is made, everything seems to be in its proper place, and she has her own adjoining washroom. But there's a desk littered with papers and envelopes right next to her computer monitor. I was expecting something like a princess' room complete with fluffy pillows and fancy quilts, maybe a white canopy above her bed to match the white painted walls, the only colour in this entire house.

The first thing she does is excuse herself while she goes into her washroom. I guess she really was using the phone before. Or, if what Dan said is true, maybe she has to go a second time. Maybe she's got diarrhoea? What a terrible thought! How did that get into my head?

While she's taking care of matters in there, my curiosity and my legs waltz me over to her desk. I'm examining an orderly stack of letters, all addressed to 'Fissure Rock All-Teen Sports.' The return addresses are from all over the country and some are from overseas. I also notice a number of brand new video package envelopes on the desk. There is an open letter and I read from it: 'I loved watching all the action in Volume 1. Please send me Volume 2. My money order for $60 is enclosed.'

Hearing Cynthia getting ready to open the door, I move closer to her window and pretend to admire the view of her backyard.

When I actually look out down there, I am shocked once more.

She walks over to me.

Instead of turning my head I maintain its position. "Is that what I think it is?" I point to a structure on the lawn.

From behind me she wraps her arms around my upper body and rests her chin on my left shoulder. Our cheeks touch. "Yes. Danny and his friends built it."

Friends? Her brother has friends? I'm looking at a wrestling ring, complete with turnbuckles, three tightly stretched ropes and a canvas mat. How could their mother allow this object on her premises? What's next, flying pigs? My mind is taxed to the max. I'm not going to say another word about this.

Cynthia squeezes me tight in a warm hug. I'm swallowing hard as she pumps up my spirits, "That was wonderful, the way you let him win that little wrestling match."

I don't dare tell her that he had me in a hold that I really couldn't get out of.

"Anyway" I say, very eager to change the topic, "what'll we do tonight?"

"Let's just sit and talk. I want to find out who Jim Bridgeman is."

She guides me to a chair in her room, and she sits on her bed.

"Okay, but there's not much to tell." Oh great, I'm sounding as boring as I am.

Cynthia reaches to switch on the lamp at the side of her bed and flips the lampshade so the light blazes into my eyes. "Nobody escapes from my interrogations," she merrily informs me.

And I have to admit, for maybe an hour, she pulls enough answers out of me to know all the basics. I tell her how I taught myself to play guitar, by studying the dots on diagrammed chords in the songbooks of my favourite singer-composer recording artists. Blushing I relate to her my silly dream of becoming rich and famous by writing my own songs and singing them to sold-out audiences around the world. Then, without going too in-depth (not revealing what happened in the backyard of my so-called friend when I was eight), I disclose that I was bullied in school, treating it more like a general afterthought. I add that, as time went by, I became more popular thanks to my soccer and swimming exploits. When my parents told me we'd be moving up here, I figured life is full of changes, no big deal. However I can't seem to find where I fit in the universe, or more precisely right here in Fissure Rock. All this, and more, I tell her.

She listens patiently, asking all the right follow-up questions to get the most out of me.

It feels good to get it off my chest. The whole time I'm talking, I just can't believe I'm here with her. "What about you?" I say. "What makes Cynthia Sacalla tick?"

We're both startled as the front door downstairs opens and people enter the house noisily. We leave her room to find out what's going on.

ON THE MAIN LEVEL two people are talking loudly in the kitchen, where we're headed.

One of the voices is very familiar, "When he agreed to the price of my initial quote, I had to tell you!" Excessive laughter follows his comment.

By the time Cynthia and I step into the kitchen, Sally Sacalla and my dad are practically doubled over in laughing spasms.

"Hey kids! How are you?" Sally spouts out with glee. She's drunk as a skunk like the old saying goes.

Cynthia smiles, "Hi, Mom. Coffee?" She begins making it without waiting for an answer.

My dad, also highly inebriated, yells out, "This is my son, Sally! I don't mean his name is Sally!" They're both splitting a gut over that one. "Well, you know what I mean!"

For the first time ever, I look at my Dad and see an idiot. This is an alarming scene to witness. All I can think is . . . what the hell is going on?

Sally exclaims, "Of course! I met Jim the first day you moved up here. How are you, hon'?"

I have to say something. "Dad, we all thought you were working." The serious expression on my face is there on purpose. I'm angry.

Smiling at me with blood-shot eyes, he stumbles, "W-w-we were."

Sally butts in, "Yeah, we were having a few drinks with a client." Unlike my Dad, she is able to chat without wobbling her words. "And guess what?" Sally turns to her coffee-making daughter.

On cue Cynthia grins, giving her mother the words she's waiting for, "You closed the deal." She begins pouring coffee into two big mugs.

"Exactly!" Dad erupts in a glow of happiness. I've never seen him silly happy. I've never seen him drunk. "Sally, your daughter is brilliant. Holy smokes, my son and her are friends already, just like us. This is a wonderful surprise, Jim!"

Outraged, that's what I am at the moment. How dare my father come into another woman's house after a night of drinking instead of going home to his wife! Cynthia scans my eyes briefly. She senses my raw feelings and asks me what my father takes in his coffee.

"Nothing," I mutter in disgust.

Sally exclaims, "There's my little munch-kin!"

Dan has joined the party.

Dad tries to show off his good memory. "Don't tell me. This must be Danny!"

All three of us correct him, "Dan!"

The air in this kitchen is filled with alcohol fumes. They make me decide to never take up drinking.

"All right, you two," Cynthia addresses both adults, "follow Dan into the family room and drink your coffee." She hands the mugs to her brother and he dutifully carries them down the hallway with Sally and Dad in tow. "Jim and I are going for a short walk."

WE'RE OUTSIDE, and I'm frazzled. "I can't believe this! It's almost 9:30! My mom's thinking he's working late and it turns out he's been drinking, having a whale of a time with a woman who's supposed to be his boss!"

Cynthia locks her hand into mine, and we commence to walk toward Fissure Rock's main street. "You're kind of cute when you're mad," she teases, showing a flash of teeth. More soberly she says, "Listen, my mom drinks a lot, okay? She also runs a very successful real estate business, the only one in town. Your father could be drinking with worse people."

I breathe in deeply. "You mean I have to accept this is as part of his job?"

She nods quietly as a couple of cars carrying loud, wild and very high teenagers whoosh by us. Everybody's stimulated tonight.

ROCK EIGHT

ONCE HE'S PARTIALLY SOBER, I walk home with my father. The conversation is not like our ordinary ones; it's stilted, superficial. We're both embarrassed by the goings-on of this evening and as soon as we walk through the front door, I lie to Mom about how he and I just happened to bump into each other while I was on my way back from Cynthia's. She thinks that's nice.

Popping my head into the living room, I am confronted with Lisa's 'don't mess with me' glance while she pretends to be absorbed by the TV. The oversized black clothes she's wearing match her hideous personality.

I fly up the stairs and hide in my room. My alarm clock tells me it's midnight. Off with my clothes, I slide under the covers of my bed. After everything I've been through tonight, I can't imagine drifting off to dreamland right away.

What's up with Dad? Is it all as simple as he and Sally made it sound? He's acting very . . . different. And what's with those video orders on Cynthia's desk? What kind of "action" was on Volume 1? As soon as I begin thinking of all the possibilities, I try to put an end to it. I know Cynthia better than that. No, there must be reasonable explanations to all the questions running through my crazy little head. I'm sure to find out the truth, and when I finally do I'll laugh about all these asinine assumptions of mine. It takes forever to lose consciousness. Thankfully I have a dreamless sleep.

SATURDAY MORNING. I'm up at the first sight of light, slithering quietly downstairs to the kitchen. I munch on a small bowl full of something-or-other cereal, then search through the phone book to find an address. Because the temperature has plunged, I put on my jacket prior to plodding out there. Realizing it's way too early to knock on somebody's door, I head towards Main Street to see if anything's kicking at this time of day. As expected my eyes are haunted by ghost town scenery, except for Lynda's Home Cooking. I've passed by this restaurant before, what Mom refers to as a greasy spoon. Now I decide to push the envelope by pulling on the door marked 'OPEN' and walking in.

Older people sit in the smoke-smoggy place. A guy in his late sixties perches on a barstool at the counter, wearing a red-and-black plaid jacket. His fat unshaven face looks like rough sandpaper, and his large nose is hooked to one side. Between rapid gulps of steak, eggs, toast and coffee, he takes powerful drags on a smouldering cigarette. He chats with Lynda in a deep gurgling voice that you think could use a good throat clearing, but his repeated rounds of violent coughing don't fix the rattle.

He says to her, "Geez, Lyn, when is it you and me are goin' out anyhow?"

"Does the word 'never' mean anything to you, Renaldo?"

O, heavy rejection! He responds with a devil-like laugh. This sets me to wondering if the man's name actually is Renaldo or if she's just being funny. You don't picture these local farmer and truck-driver types with fancy names like that. Much more popular are one-syllable identifiers like: Bob, Ed, Tom and so on.

I settle in a seat at a table next to a slightly opened window that allows me to breathe more freely. Amazingly, considering it's so early, the place is about half full. They're chattering to each other, while I'm comfortable blending into the wood grain of the tabletop listening to static country music playing on the old grease-coated radio beside the grill.

"Hi-ya, Sunshine!" Lynda has discovered a new stray on her premises, and it's me. "Kind-a neat to see a fresh face 'round here!" She's one of those shiny morning people, grinding away at a big wad of gum in her mouth and holding a steaming coffee pot in her hand.

"Hello," I say without enthusiasm.

"Good-looking boy like you can do better than that!" Lynda jokingly scolds me, and when I don't respond it's down to business. "What'll you have?"

"Orange juice, please."

"Glass of vitamin C comin' right up!" Off she goes.

Nobody takes any notice of me. I'm able to kill time by thinking through my plan in peace. Lately things have been slowly but surely slipping away from me. Okay, Mrs. Arseneault was right about practically everything she said during that dreadful school meeting with my mother and me. Still there remains one wonderful error. She was dead wrong concerning Cynthia, because she really does like me! 'And yes, Mrs. Arseneault, just like you said, I can use Cynthia as a peer model to get my schoolwork up to par.'

I pull out a pen and a small pad from the big side pocket of my jacket and begin scribbling down lyrics to another song. Naturally Cynthia is the subject matter. However I have to add some fictional details, like pretending we live together (he-he). With such pleasant imagery in mind I take my time relishing it. Making changes, I finally find the proper lyrics that make the scene click for me.

> She has a talent to draw in the morning
> She has sketches that say the right thing
> I get angry when my toast gets burned
> And she laughs, as the birds sing
>
> The world is her oyster and fortune
> The world is her string of fine pearls
> I get bogged down with my struggles
> And she is the best of all worlds

BY 9:00 I'M WALKING BACK along Main Street. The retail spots begin opening for business in orderly succession, dominoes falling in slow motion. I continue composing in my mind, committing the new lyrics to memory. A tune makes its way in my head. When I get back home, I'll use my guitar to find the chords that'll fit with it.

> Feelings so strong
> Swing in the breeze
> Nothing is wrong
> When you aim to please
>
> There is an afternoon bustle about her
> There is the welcoming dance of her ways
> I get lonely when we're parted
> And she brings meaning to my days

BRIGHT SPEARS OF SUNLIGHT bounce off car and store windows, stinging my eyes as I walk northwest in search of Shroud Circle. I've resolved to carry out my mission. This is by far the wealthiest street in town, although you can't really call any of these houses mansions—I don't think Fissure Rock has such an animal. All in all, number 7 does put our own house in town to shame. I ring the doorbell anyway.

Andy arrives, opens the heavy oak door and stands in the impressive front foyer. "Jim!" He's in a happy mood. "Are you lost?"

"I, uh . . . ." Oh, God! I know exactly why I'm here . . . it's kind of difficult to express. "I didn't . . . do a very good job yesterday when I said I was sorry. Can I explain?"

Andy laughs, not at me, but with a kind of laugh sweeping all the bad stuff away in seconds. "You came here, so you must be sorry." Is there a double-meaning in his words? Mimicking an old-fashioned English butler he says, "If you will be so kind as to follow me, sir."

"Thanks." I'm overwhelmed by his easy forgiveness before noticing the lavish interior of his house. His folks must be loaded.

"Any plans for today?"

"No," I say.

"Great, my parents left me alone for the whole day. I was

going to do the suicide thing and now I can't. They say that's impolite when you've got company." Andy sure is showing a morbid sense of humour.

Playing his straight man I add, "Don't mean to throw a wrench into your plans."

"Ah," he sighs, "all is forgotten. Want to hang out with me for a while?"

I think Andy's a pretty good friend to have. I'm treated to a grand tour of this upper-class house. There's no sense getting into dry details; every room and hallway is immaculate, absolutely outdoing Cynthia's awesome abode. Before he shows me the final room I tell him I don't care what this place costs, I'll buy it! We share a short guffaw over my enthusiasm.

"Here's something I think you'll like." Andy pauses with his hand on the knob. He opens the door, majestically, and walks in.

Following I can see we are in a large room with a swimming pool. Three big skylights in the ceiling make up for windowless walls. Down on my knees by the side of the pool, I swish my hand in the water. The temperature is perfect for my liking. "Too bad I didn't bring my bathing suit," I remark.

"No one else's here. I'm a lonely only child." Andy coughs one time and says, "Let's swim anyway."

"Skinny-dipping?"

His face turns red when I look at him. "What?" He looks scared. "No, no!" Smiling uncomfortably, Andy rattles on, "I've got lots of bathing suits! You can borrow one."

"Okay," I shrug, wondering why he's acting so strange about nothing.

He shows me where the change room is and hands a spare swimming suit to me. Then he goes up to his room to get his own.

By the time I'm walking towards the pool deck, he's standing on the diving board preparing to enter the water. Talk about a quick-change artist.

"Hey Jim!" Andy shouts from the diving board. "You're the expert. Check this out!" With that he bounces high up and somersaults into the water. Down deep he glides, drifting up to the surface. Revealing a hopeful expression he asks, "How was that?"

I have to respond quickly. He wants my approval. "I'd say a nine. Ten is nearly impossible to get."

"Your turn," he says.

Humouring him, I do the exact same dive. Hitting the water, my skin prickles in long-awaited sensations that I haven't enjoyed since leaving the city. I swim likewise underwater, and when I break to the top I splash away at a backstroke for a couple of widths of the pool. "Awesome," I conclude, treading water.

"I give you an eight," he teases.

"Prejudicial judging! I demand an appeal."

This is cool, the way we're lightly ribbing each other.

He reminds me, "Ten is just about impossible, and nine is mine."

"Nine would make us equal."

Andy shakes his head. "Naw, we can't have a tie. Somebody has to win."

Almost seriously, I ask, "Why?"

"Because." He practically beams.

Nodding I chortle, "Now that's good reasoning. You'll make a great parent someday."

At this, his jaw drops in mock shock.

I swim to the ledge and pull myself out of the pool. We automatically start walking to the diving board again. This time, I loop ahead of him to dive first.

As I step out onto the board Andy says, "You didn't take my advice about Cynthia, did you?"

Well, I'm so surprised I almost topple off the edge for a truly crappy dive. "No. But we're just friends." Why do I need to give him an explanation?

"Yeah, I suppose certain people are impossible to resist." Face blank, he peers at me.

I'd really like to ask him, 'Just what exactly is this terrible thing about Cynthia?' But some unknown force holds me back.

I remember what Cynthia said at the Falls and, thinking it will ease the situation, I inform Andy, "She told me she thinks you're a real sweet guy."

"Anything else?" His eyes are full of gloom.

"Nope." I throw all my energy into a terrific dive to shake off this tense moment and my own nagging curiosity about what once went on between Cynthia and Andy.

WE DON'T DO MUCH MORE than another ten minutes of diving and swimming, because he's tired out. Andy throws a towel at me while he goes into a corner and pulls out two plastic chairs that recline so we can stretch out on them. Before long we're sipping ice tea, pretending it's summertime and watching—through one skylight directly above us—the red and yellow leaves rattle on the branches of their mother trees in the cool wind. I stare at the glimmering pool and rest my eyes just for a second, immersed in the warmth of these surroundings. We are temporarily cheating the season . . . an illusion.

"Andy?"

"Yup." His eyes are half-closed as he lies in his chair, looking at me.

"Do you really want to move to the city?"

He doesn't flinch. Again, those big brown eyes look into my green peepers. "What I want makes zero difference." His stare continues.

"You've lived in Fissure Rock all your life. I guess you'll miss it, huh?"

Andy's eyebrows rise. "Oh, maybe just you and your crazy questions." He puts on a weak smile.

There is a long silence.

From a far away place he asks, "You want a back rub?"

"What?" I heard exactly what he said. (I can't believe it, though.) Is Andy . . . ?

"Do you . . ." and he starts laughing like a madman, "want me . . ." (He has to stop cold for half a minute and by this time

I'm laughing with him.) " . . . to give you . . . a back rub?" He's in spasms like a wild animal caught in a trap; I lag cautiously behind.

After our laughter dies down, I think of a good firm answer. "Definitely not."

"Fine," he acknowledges, as though I'd given him the only possible response. Andy is back in control of himself, and I'm relieved. "Before my idiocy took charge of me, what were you talking about?"

"About moving. Have you told your parents how you feel about it?" At times, I'm as curious as my old cat.

Reaching down to sip from the straw in his ice tea, Andy frowns thoughtfully and shakes his head. "My conversations with dear mother and father are completely off limits. Nothing personal."

"Fine with me." It's like I never know the right thing to say, as I fall silent looking at the constantly shifting surface of the pool.

ROCK NINE

AFTER HAVING A LATE LUNCH with Andy, and playing a few video games with him on his computer, I leave. Finding myself empty on the deserted school football field, I feel a nervous energy I want to get rid of. By this time, late afternoon clouds have sneaked across the sky while I wasn't paying attention. Swimming inside 7 Shroud Circle was so-so. Most of the visit was spent happily lounging on a chair, talking with my soon-to-be-departing friend. Now I need real exercise. It comes in a sudden surge. Immediately my legs seize control of me and I am off and racing along the gravel chips of the running track. I haven't had a haircut since before moving up here, and my thick blond waves are billowing from both sides of my head as I run directly into the autumn wind slapping my face.

    I'm trying with everything I've got to not think at all. I only want to feel. Faster I pound, driving my feet for higher acceleration, willing my lungs and heart to work harder. My inner heat pops out through pores in my skin, quickly cooled by outside air. This is something I can do: zip around this circle at a wicked pace, not getting anywhere, but feeling it. And I am deeply into what I'm doing, that's what I feel, capturing a moment and taking action with an atom of time.

    Four laps make a mile. I do not stop my determined dash until I've counted eight. In a flash, two miles have gone by. Doubled over, winded, streaming with sweat, I clutch my knees and squeeze while working to get my breath back. My gaze is fixed on the pebbled track. Tiny droplets of perspiration roll down my face and splash soundlessly onto stone chips. Bits and pieces, I think to myself. Bits and pieces are what we are, and later, dust to dust. These depressing thoughts sink back into me after a relaxing day at Andy's and even after rushing like a wild horse, forcing the endorphins to flow through my bloodstream.

Bitter and weary, I trudge home in the looming dusk. What the hell's wrong with me?

WALKING INSIDE MY HOUSE, I see that Lisa is helping Mom set the table for dinner. This isn't abnormal. She's known to help out around the house if it gets her something she wants. Even her choice of clothes is more acceptable. Likely she's working on a raise in her allowance. Who knows and who cares? Of course I say hi to Mom while she busies herself in the kitchen; she hopes I've had a good day; I say, yeah, yeah.

Making my way to the living room, I notice Dad on the couch with his head back and eyes closed.

I sit down on a chair opposite, cross my arms and observe my father and the growing darkness outside the window behind him. True I must stink something fierce. So what?

Turns out he was only half-asleep. I frown as he raises his head and opens the eyes on his pale face. "Hey, kid. How goes it?"

"Couldn't be better," and I don't budge.

"Your desk shows some homework piling up on you again." Been snooping around my room, has he? This is too much! His charming, cheerful voice doesn't fool me for a second. He, the guilty party, is attempting to weasel his way out by making me the fall guy. Well it isn't going to work!

Not missing a beat to even blink my eyes, I slam-dunk him with: "At least I'm not the one who got smashed last night."

He puts his hand on his head. "Please, Jim. I'm still serving my hangover punishment today." Is this a plea for sympathy? He'll get none from me.

Lisa enters and calmly says, "Hey, you two, dinner."

Hmm, I'm wondering how long she'll be playing her game.

HALFWAY THROUGH THE MEAL I am almost certain that

my family has been kidnapped and replaced by impostors. Lisa's super-nice to Dad. She can't do enough for him: want some more of this, more of that? This is the man she supposedly despises. Mom wears a proud expression on her face while watching my sister going through the motions of a 'nice' new attitude. Dad's pretending nothing happened last night. And none of them are talking to me. They're completely nuts!

My fuse finally reaches its end as I say, "Am I invisible or something?"

Mom knits her brows at me. "That's an odd thing to ask, darling."

I'm given no answer.

Oh, I can always count on Dad to throw in a little more. "We figured you'd tell us in your own good time, son." He begins sprinkling pepper on his squash.

Of all people Lisa helps unravel my confusion. "You left this morning before anybody got up, so they've been worried all day about where you were." She says this in such an even, mature tone, I can't believe my ears. "Maybe you could've left them a note, or called from wherever you were?"

There is a kind of conspiracy in the air; they've all ganged up on me. To hell with it, I won't tell them a thing!

IN MY ROOM AFTER DINNER, sorting through books and papers on my desk, I'm thinking over my normal policy which has always been to please my folks—and even Lisa. When she was really little I used to be able to make her giggle all the time. I'd make funny faces or do stupid voices and stuff, and she'd be killing herself. Anyway I'm re-examining that policy as I sift about trying to figure out what's what. I know I have a test in some subject on Monday. At school it's in one ear and out the other. Sure I scribble down notes, hard not to when a teacher peers over my shoulder like a goddamn vulture. But looking at my ink scrawls once I'm home I can't make any connection. My interest level is about zilch. Honestly I try my best for my parents but they've been letting me down lately, especially Dad with his new late-night antics. The dinner situation was another example. Everyone's become hidden behind pleasantries. If they wanted to know where I was, why the hell didn't they ask? Screw them.

"A BONFIRE?" I repeat loudly into the mouthpiece.

Cynthia has just called me from her cell phone, inviting me out. "It's French, Jim. Means 'good fire.'" (Funny girl.)

Everything has happened so fast I don't know what to say. Before she called I showered away my sprint sweat, so I'm primed to go. "I wouldn't mind."

Mom's in the kitchen with me. Out of character she jabs her index finger in the direction of my face to make her point more dramatic, "You're not going anywhere, young man, until I see your homework's done." Oh yeah, she's serious.

"I heard that," Cynthia's voice asserts into my ear. "Tell her I'm coming over to help you with it."

"Why?" I ask.

"Because I am." She disconnects.

A FEW MINUTES DRAG ON, then the girl of my dreams is in my room. "Okay, let's see what we can do." Like an executive secretary on an overdose of diet pills, she gathers up papers from my desk, puts them in file folders, labels each one by subject and writes down assignment due dates for me. Cynthia even discovers that my test on Monday is in Science. The whole process couldn't have taken more than fifteen minutes. Wow, I'm organized now. Finally she calls down in the sweetest voice imaginable to my mother. "Oh, Mrs. Bridgeman?"

Mom and Dad both come up.

"He does have a desk under there!" my father jokes. He tries to be so witty.

My mother's more subdued. "Looks good, but can you keep it this way?" Her blinding spotlight eyes catch me by surprise.

Before I can respond Cynthia speaks, "He promised me he would and I said, if he doesn't, I won't see him anymore. I don't date failing students."

We are dating! It's official. Cynthia just confirmed it.

Dad reacts, "That would be a stiff penalty, dear, don't you think?"

"Hmm," Mom muses. She's still not keen on the idea.

Once again nobody's talking to me. They're all commenting about me. I am getting tired of this treatment. In fact it's really beginning to piss me off. Do they not see I'm in the same room as they are, namely my room? Need I say more? I say nothing.

The deal here is that Cynthia wants me to go to this bonfire, and I'll go next to anywhere to be with her. We're apparently trying to convince my parents that I can start on my homework tomorrow (Sunday). After all, everything on my desk is in its place and ready to be tackled. However Mom is taking a much longer time than usual making up her mind. Dad's vote doesn't really count; my mother arbitrarily decides these kinds of things. She's acting kind of strange.

First she looks at me and frowns—the devil she knows and can't help but love (he-he). Her gaze then focuses on my new girlfriend. It seems stuck on her forever. There is a trace of disapproval in Mom's eyes, something close to hatred and it really creeps me out. Plainly even Cynthia's slightly on edge as she glances at me, bravely holding onto her smile.

"All right," my mother finally concedes, but there's no doubt she's somehow going against her better judgment. She stands still as a concrete statue.

Cynthia explodes with enormous celebration and embraces Mom. "Oh, thank you, Mrs. B. You're the greatest!" My mother is unmoved by this lively show of affection.

The greatest what? I wonder coldly.

I AM AN UNHAPPY PASSENGER in the car belonging to Cynthia's mother. Am I a tad envious because it's a BMW and I'm not the one who's driving? Naw, those kinds of things don't bother me. Perhaps I remain angered by Mom's hard-edged attitude? Wrong again; I've blocked her from my mind. It's because Cynthia's brother is in the back seat! I hadn't counted on a midget chaperon. She explains to me that this big bonfire event is where a lot of Dan's friends will also be, and so on and so forth. Okay so that's the trade-off, I guess. Better than staying at home doing nothing. We are cruising toward the highway and the Falls is our target.

It's quiet in the car on the way up and only a short drive. Cynthia parks with the other cars on grassy picnic grounds, level with the lake. As we get out I notice the weather is turning cooler at night and I anticipate a first snowfall soon. Partying sounds from other kids are nearby. We walk along the black shore of the lake, and I'm amazed that neither she nor her brother needs a flashlight to see where we're going. Cynthia carries a large bag; she won't let me carry it for her. I follow them up a dirt and stone slope to the same area where my first kiss with Cynthia had taken place.

A large bonfire is at full burn and around it about twenty kids are gathered whose faces I vaguely recognize from school. Leaping tongues of light alternate with darkness, and my flame-blurred vision makes out these coming-and-going faces through the crazily flickering fire. Beer bottles are plenty, everywhere, full and empty. Laughter echoes all around the tiny lake's granite walls. I make up my mind (as everyone welcomes Cynthia) that I am going to enjoy myself. I will fit in. To hell with it, I'm no different than anyone else.

A guy, who sits on a log with a girl propped under his arm, shouts out at me, "Hey there, Bridgeman! Sink any baskets lately?" Bellowing out a jack-ass laugh, he's quite proud of himself over that one, and his monkey-see-monkey-do compatriots do the same. I'm no good with names . . . I know he's in my gym class . . . and on the school basketball team.

Smiling back I shake my head, "Not that lucky." No point in taking offence.

Dan has found friends from his grade, and they're having their little party away from the rest of us. Cynthia is doing her best to humour her many friends and hangers-on, each of whom need to talk with her immediately, as usual.

I'm left standing around alone, wondering what to do next. Basically I wait for my girlfriend (we're dating now, she said so) to return to me. On the other hand I also have to become more self-resourceful, strive towards an outgoing and social personality. Great. So how do you begin doing that? Where's the instruction manual? These kids all know each other, but they don't know me. Sure, they've seen my face around and some (like the basketball guy) even know my name. That's it, though. Out of nowhere I ask myself, 'Where are the marshmallows to roast?' Then I think back at what a stupid thought that is. We're all in high school. Beer and joints have replaced the childish shit. Is this what Lisa meant when she said I should grow up?

Moving closer to the cliff edge above the lake, I feel the steady warmth from the fire massage my back. Taking this in for a few deep breaths, I begin to feel more relaxed. Some male on the beach below is taking a piss into the water. I'm not impressed. Let's say I want to swim in this lake next summer. All I'll be thinking about is how this twit had contaminated it with his urine. Gross! I turn away and face the fire.

Minutes later, back up with the rest of us, the pissing guy approaches me. Don't tell me he's going to say something menacing like, 'What were you looking at me for?' There's always that kind of talk going on at school, both here and back in the city (universal insinuations, accusations). This time I'm spared any such crap. "You're . . . Jim?" He's taller than me, has dark features, and extends his hand for a shake.

Branches in the fire spit and crackle as I try to decide what to do. I'm damn sure he didn't wash his hands. Even if he had swished them about in the lake it wouldn't have done much good, since he'd just finished pissing in it. Quick thinker I am, a coughing fit causes me to cover my mouth with both hands and I hack away for quite awhile. By the time I've 'recovered,' he's withdrawn his hand. "Yeah," I finally answer his question, and I even pat him on the shoulder of his jacket. After all, I'm trying to expand my circle of friends by mixing with these fellow creatures. "Sorry, though, I don't know your—"

"Joe," he interjects. "I've seen you and Cynthia hanging around. Any friend of hers gets a free sample." He hasn't shaven in a few days and it really shows on him. He pulls out a small clear plastic bag; inside are a few pre-rolled joints.

I've been in this situation before at my old school. I smoked pot once and I did inhale. It wound up that I didn't get high at all. Later, someone told me that the first time doesn't always give you a buzz anyway. "Um," I react, and I admit I'm thinking over his offer. "Not right now."

Joe reveals friendly and crooked yellow teeth. "No prob, bro. What-cha need's an appetizer." He points to an open box snuggled between two birch trees. "Over there's my stash o' beer. If you got ten bucks on you, go grab yerself a few."

Why not? Everyone else is drinking, chatting, milking the moment for all it's worth. Dad gets a kick out of splitting a beer with me now and then, too, though it tastes bitter to tell the truth. I shell out two fives and hand them to him. "Thanks," I say to Joe. I start walking toward the bottles that wait for me. "Thanks a lot."

"Hey," he replies, "what I'm here for."

I'm actually kind of thirsty; probably that's why the beer tastes good. Returning to my spot by the fire, bottle in hand, I can't see Joe or Cynthia anywhere. Music from a boom box has begun to play and there's a big cheer to greet it. Some of the gang are already up and dancing. After awhile I'm kind of tapping one foot and moving my shoulders in time to the beat. Things are starting to unwind. Bending my head back to stare at the stars splattered on the sky, I release a short laugh, knowing that I am in a place and at a time that feels just right inside my bones.

More and more often I go between those birch trees to get more beer, and everyone is becoming friendlier towards me. An hour passes, I think. Then another? I enjoy some mindless chat with other kids and they seem pleased by my presence. My girlfriend isn't the only person who has charisma! Not keeping track, I can only guess that I'm drinking bountifully from bottle number five at the same moment Cynthia crosses my mind. Joe wanders about in the distance, talking to people, and occasionally gesturing thumbs-up at me in an old pal kind of way.

Deciding to look for Cynthia I start off where I saw Dan and his friends go, by the opening of the path leading into the woods. He and his buddies are there inside a circled patch of loose sand, next to a small grassy area. Although difficult to see I can make out Dan's face as belonging to one of the bodies in this sandpit frantically moving around, up and down, play fighting. Angry shouting and different types of laughter collide. Because I haven't been noticed yet, I stand silently and let my eyes soak in what is unfolding before them.

A dark figure rushes my way. I'm alarmed at first, thinking it could be a bear or anything. Squinting my eyes I see it's just a boy (apparently one of Dan's friends). The closer he gets the more scared his face looks. His shirt is all ripped to pieces, his eyes are brimming with tears, and he races past me like he's running away from a ghost. From where Dan is the calls follow him, "Don't forget, Phil, you don't tell nobody!" and "Remember, nothing happened!" What the hell was that about?

Back in the sandpit, Dan is in control. Everyone who comes his way is promptly picked up and tossed to the ground. He regularly bellows victoriously into the cool mid-October air: "You can't beat me!" or "I'm undefeatable!" or something like that. A few of his opponents are bigger than him, not to mention bigger than me. I'm sad for his friends. Yeah, most are messing around as if it means nothing, but some of them (maybe like the one who just blitzed by me) must secretly feel like pitiful powerless pawns in Dan's wrestling kingdom. I know why no one can beat him, and it isn't because he's stronger than the rest. None of them has the guts to challenge Dan's claim as the one in charge; that's how he gets to keep his crown. He has an ancient killer instinct branded into him. If it's possible to wear something like that well . . . then Dan is succeeding.

Even just playing about, as these fourteen-year-olds are, I'd hate to lose. On the flip side of the coin, even just fooling around, I could never see myself knocking down anybody's pride by being some cocky winner.

Dan's getting great pleasure out of this activity. One by one, he shows off his 'skills' (scoop-slams, suplexes, pile-drivers, power-bombs, whatever). I continue to watch, fascinated, as the music from the bonfire area reverberates and conversations linger from the older others nearby. Shadowy though it appears through this night-time visibility, the smile on Dan's face is remarkable. You usually consider smiles as warm and welcoming, or sometimes sarcastic and threatening. Dan's smile conveys a clear-cut primal thirst that is being repeatedly quenched. And still he wants more. It seems like he'll never tire of this thrill to win; it's everything to him. His desire is embedded in hungry sparkling eyes.

I wonder what the feeling is like . . . having complete control over someone else. To be in Dan's position—the boss-man, the indestructible one—is what I want right now. It'll never happen for me, I know, because how can you change your personality? I don't have his killer instinct. At the same time I'm ashamed, and rebuke myself for having this evil little wish in the first place. With these mixed feelings, I ache in a sudden cold autumn wind.

"Jim, is that you?" Dan, the hunter, has spotted me during a lull in his sandpit wrestling promotion.

Reminding myself why I've strayed from the warm comfort of the bonfire, I say, "Yeah, I'm looking for your sister. Seen her?"

"She's—" and he looks behind him at the backdrop of trees.

Did I just see a tiny red light quickly going out, in there? We both hear something scrambling away; sounds to me like a raccoon. A one-eyed, red-eyed raccoon?

Dan turns back to face me. "Well, she's around somewhere."

They return to their play fighting as I ponder my search for Cynthia. I simply go back to action central, the bonfire itself. She's bound to show up eventually. First I make a beeline for the bottled brews between birch trees. That's where Joe is, and he slings an arm around my shoulder.

"Whoa, Bridgeman," he says in a super-relaxed way. "We can't have ya drinkin' me dry." Joe shows those less-than-perfect teeth of his.

Again the wind picks up, and a cold rustle of leaves chills me. I'm feeling pretty damn good, though, after about five beers. "Sorry, Joe, I'm being a leech." I plan to walk away and over near the bonfire flames that dance wild in the dead night air.

Joe takes his arm off me, and from his pocket fishes out the joints. "It's time for the good stuff, guy." He lights one up.

There's no reason to explain anything. I go ahead and smoke up with him, except tonight I do catch a buzz. It takes some time for the sensations to seep through. Sure beats beer. After we've toked, he guides me over to the bonfire area and I sit down on a log. I'm doing great . . . no worries at all to cloud my head. Everything seems crystal clear and just as it should be. The world is a fine and perfect place to live in. This moment has been frozen in time . . . somehow I feel so light.

Before he leaves me, Joe whispers into my ear, "Hey, don't forget where you got this stuff, okay?"

"Thanks," I say, "I absolutely won't." I don't even try to suppress the big wide grin on my face . . . just let it happen . . . open up.

Joe laughs, "Absolutely won't! I like that," and he stalks his way somewhere else. "You're all right, Bridgeman!" He's on the hunt for additional customers, figuring I'm already a new one after having just supplied me with free samples.

After he's gone, I stare for I-don't-know-how-long into the scorching heat of the bonfire. People talk to me, names and faces aren't important. They're . . . 'nice' as Mom would say (I laugh out loud, imagining her facial expression if she could see me here and now). I can't connect with any of the conversations, despite me being a part of them. It's all small talk. Another human gives me a sixth beer, just for being the sweet-looking guy I am, I suppose, and I drink it all up. I'm floating, seated on the cold and strangely comfortable log.

Tap, tap, tap on my shoulder. Someone's finger. I look around for its owner. Cynthia! She smiles at me, then frowns as I smile in return. Mine is too exaggerated for her liking.

"Jim, you're totally stoned." Her voice betrays a mild disappointment.

"Yes," I sing as if it's a wonderful thing. Finally I burst out laughing.

She waits for my outburst to subside, then calls Dan over.

As soon as he obeys, his clothing covered in sand like a four-year-old, Cynthia tells him we're going home. She picks up the large bag she came here with and does some quick good-byes to her friends around the bonfire.

We begin to walk down the slope along the beach, and I take a fast look back, stopping suddenly in my tracks. From a fair distance I see faces at the tops of the flames. Not the kids who are really there partying but ghostly Native peoples' faces, their weary mist-filled eyes smothered in smoky sadness. And I'm shocked by how much misery is in those eyes. I feel guilty, as a contributor to the desecration of their sacred spot. Naturally it's got to be an illusion of sorts. My drugged state of mind is playing tricks on me. Cynthia and Dan each grab an arm and drag me onward, to the picnic grounds where Cynthia's mother's BMW is parked.

IN THE BACK SEAT I pay close attention during the short ride home. Wordless, because I'm wasted, my ears pick up Dan and Cynthia's private talk. With one shoulder and my head slouched against the side window, I pretend to be asleep.

"Did you get it all?" That's Dan demanding.

"I think so. We'll see later."

"Let's dump him off first."

Cynthia bristles at this suggestion. "Don't be crazy. I met his mother tonight."

Her brother thinks that's funny. "So? Since when do you care—?"

"Think of it as good public relations, bro," she sermonizes. "We have to sober him up before he's in any shape to face her."

Dan's throwing a quasi-tantrum. "Well I wanna see—"

"You will," she assures him sternly. "We have to do things in the right order."

"All right," he finally agrees. "All's I know is I won all my matches!"

The lid of my left eye opens just enough to observe Cynthia's profile as she smiles at him in a special big-sister manner. "I've never seen you lose." Then her gaze is fixed on the road. She's a careful driver.

Questions jump into my hazy head. Was that Cynthia hiding in the woods filming Dan's sandpit activities? If so, why? Are they keeping me in the dark about something? Too stoned to analyze further, I drop my search for an answer.

ROCK TEN

MORNING BRINGS CLOUDY RECALL of me being in Cynthia's house again, with those blinding white walls everywhere; of Dan leaving us to go up to his room; of her practically forcing coffee down my throat. How long had I been there? What was said between us? Don't know. I was thankful when she drove me home and we both discovered that my parents had already gone to bed. She helped me with my key to open the front door and left. I'm just about sure that was all.

My eyes finally open. First thing I see is an itsy-bitsy spider crawling upside-down on the ceiling. Really I don't have anything special against these eight-legged creatures; got to admit, they weave some wicked webs. Still I'm feeling awfully queasy as I watch this life-form from above slowly creep down the wall right beside me, where I lie in bed. 'Spider, spider, on the wall . . . who's the most messed up of all? Sorry, Spidey, you lose.' Reaching for and then rolling up one of my music magazines (it was going to get thrown out anyway), I give the arthropod a fatal smack. Next I toss the newly soiled periodical into the trashcan. The smear formerly known as Spider is gone.

I force my legs out from under the covers and plant one foot at a time on the floor. After assuming the sitting position I'm on some merry-go-round, spinning not-so-merrily on a spot in my room. And I've got a sledgehammer of a headache to boot. Even bigger trouble's brewing ahead for me if Mom finds out I'd been drinking (and-God-knows-what-else) last night.

But this first hangover of mine isn't enough. Oh no, not by a long shot. I begin coughing, sneezing and reaching for the old tissue box to blow my runny nose. An impish grin slides onto my face. Don't get me wrong, I hate getting colds, but this here just might cover up nicely the hangover evidence. I could pretend this cold is the flu and win myself some major slack. It's worth a try. Rather than finding fresh clothes, I simply put on a clean pair of socks and wear my bathrobe down to the kitchen.

Mom looks up from the stove where she's cooking pancakes. My stomach is now getting very sickly. She speaks, redirecting my attention, "Jim, were you making all that noise upstairs?"

After a quick glance at the table, where Dad and Lisa are seated, I realize she's baited me with another minnow from her stream of frivolous questions. In my head I say, 'No, Mom, it was the bears.' Well, I can't actually afford to start being sarcastic at this point so I reply, "Yup." I play it to the hilt by slowly sitting down beside Lisa and putting my hands against the sides of my head. "Oh, ugh," I moan.

"I feel exactly the same way about you!" Lisa snaps at me. At least she's back to normal.

Dad wisely ignores her and states mildly, "Quite a late night you had, son."

Before either of my parents can begin further probing, I sneeze unintentionally, and follow-up on purpose with a hugely exaggerated coughing spasm. Making my voice sound hoarse I say, "I feel like I'm burning up inside."

Mom rushes over with a plate full of steaming hot pancakes and places that in front of me. Her own voice is as sweet as maple syrup. "Maybe you're coming down with something. Can you eat anything?" Ma, queen of the clichés, gives me a curious look. Is she buying that I have the flu?

If anything solid gets into my system right now, I'm sure to vomit. (Too many beers last night.) Normally pancakes make up my favourite breakfast . . . shouldn't have much trouble convincing them I really must be sick if I forego it. "No thanks, Mom. I think I'll just take this orange juice with me and go back to bed. I wouldn't want Lisa to catch this."

"Hey!" the irrepressible one shouts, "don't do me any favours, dumb-ass!"

I laugh a little inside myself. Honestly I would not want Lisa to get my cold. Can you imagine trying to live with her being twice as cranky as she is usually? Non, mérci.

Mom takes exception to her gnarly remark. "Let me remind you, young lady, that your continued internet privileges are connected to your improved behaviour in this household."

Pushing myself up from the table, I am really proud of my mother's well worded warning. I'm sure that Mr. King would herald it as a good example of "parallelism." And it works like magic. Lisa is suddenly silent as stone; Dad says nothing (he's slowly learning). Meanwhile I'm off the hook. I've fooled them all, at least I think I have. Maybe not. Who knows anything?

MUCH LATER AS MORNING OOZES into the afternoon, I try doing the homework thing seeing how it was so neatly organized on my desk the night before, thanks to Cynthia. Even though I can't stop sneezing and coughing, or thinking about her, I somehow plough through it. I've got to say there's no Einstein brilliance in there, but finally it's done.

I rest, stare straight ahead. One side of my desk is flush with the bottom windowsill, so I can see the first snowfall begin from the sky. Hunched over my desk, a hot cup of lemon tea in hand compliments of Mom, I'm happy that the hangover symptoms have stopped haunting me. Big popcorn flakes swirl down, leaving a shallow mid-October cover in our backyard. Surging conceit comes over me because I had practically predicted this white stuff coming on last night. I sensed it. Maybe I'm like one of the psychic locals you sometimes read about in those quirky little mystery novels.

My mind wonders about my present Fissure Rock status, specifically at school. Everyone knows Cynthia and I hang together. That's a major plus. She's by far the most popular student. Then again, I have this feeling that I'm a bit on the fringes. Last night I thought I'd made some major headway by getting to know Joe and showing the rest of the kids I'm not squeaky clean and all that. Something's out there. I said it before: I'm no dummy. Sure enough there is a game being played and I'm not in on it. Andy knows something, only he's not telling. Strange.

ROCK ELEVEN

ANOTHER WEEK SNAKES BY AT FRH and this time things appear more promising for me. First of all that cold I caught is gone in a couple of days. Also some kids who were at the bonfire stop me in the hall, before class starts, while I'm having lunch with Andy, just to say hello and ask how I'm doing. Cool. I continue to feel kind of bad for my eating partner since he's still ignored by the others. But listen, Andy's leaving soon. Like anyone else I want to have more than one friend. Cynthia is busy as ever, although she's already invited me to her big Halloween bash happening on the weekend at her place. Yeah!

"GREAT, YOU'RE EARLY!" Cynthia greets me at her front door.
The atmosphere is perfect. On her porch railing the customary mutilated pumpkins blaze spookily. Not to be outdone by the jack-o-lanterns she's dressed all in black, wearing thick orange lipstick. It's nippy out tonight, so I'm relieved to enter her house. No one else except our host Cynthia is expected to wear a real costume at this gig. We're too old for that.
"Hey Jim," says Dan mildly as he emerges from the kitchen and walks past me. He's carrying two large bowls of chips.
Before I can respond to him, Cynthia looks at his back and lays down the law. "You're not drinking tonight, Dan."
I'm waiting for a major protest out of him, but he acts like he doesn't even care. "I know." Good, he's in a calm mood for a change. This should be a fun night.
"All right, well I'm glad you know." She turns to me and pecks my cheek quickly. "How's my favourite guy?"
This stuns me. All I can think of in way of comeback is

more of my feeble humour, "Not sure. If you tell me his name, maybe I'll ask him for you."

Cynthia groans in her own confident way and gives me a light punch on the old shoulder.

From the family room, Dan starts the music blaring and now we await the arrival of everyone else.

WITHIN AN HOUR THEY'RE HERE, all sixty or so of them. I have no brain for most math things, but I'm not bad at estimating crowds. Nursing the beer in my hand, I tell myself: no way am I getting skunked tonight. Joe's already offered me some weed, and I've politely refused. There's plenty of blah-blah-blah going on and ninety-percent of everybody's eardrums is filled with heavy bass music and that's fine. I mean, it's not as if we're saying anything important, that's not the point. We're young. We're letting off steam. No one really fits in because there's nothing to fit into. I'm just like the rest of the gang. We're all hurtling through the universe on this mysterious sphere we call Earth, and no one knows why. Enough of this!

From far down the hall, somebody's voice is heard. Definitely male, it cannon balls through the competing music waves: "U-D-W!"

Cynthia and I are in the kitchen, not exactly together but in the same room at least. The other kids start filtering out, and some are nearly rushing, towards the voice. She looks at me as we are left alone for a few heartbeats. "I know it's nutty, Jim. The big Halloween Show, you know?"

Actually I don't. But we walk happily hand-in-hand into the family room, now a cluster of human bodies, all eyes fixed on the TV set. I'm anticipating a music show or something similar.

Here's what I learn: UDW stands for Universal Devastation Wrestling, the largest pro-wrestling operation on the planet. No, wait, sorry. In fact the announcer calls it: "the best and baddest wrestling federation in the entire universe!" So, for all you aliens from outer space, you have been forewarned. Packed like sardines in a small can, all the other kids are aware of each wrestler and his special gimmick.

One of the matches features the Duct-Taped Man, who inexplicably is allowed to wear duct tape wristbands with the sticky side out. This gives him a bizarre and unfair advantage over his opponents because every time he smashes them—with either one of his wrists—he peels some hair off their skin, leaving these big painful red marks. Kind of gruesome, huh?

There's this other guy called the L-Shaped Bomber. He's named after his 'finisher,' which begins with a leap off the top turnbuckle. His long legs flip up in the air like the length of the letter L. His back bends at a perfect straight angle, with arms at his sides, to form the bottom part of the L. He lands with his back on his enemy's chest and gets the pin. Very, very strange.

There are also female valets and managers. Without getting too descriptive, some of them could be magazine models. Others could be Halloween witches complete with broomsticks, or I should say a bunch of corny-ass weapons they use to taunt their men's opponents. They also physically interfere in the matches. Tough ladies!

The last match is the most memorable. It features MONEY-SPINNER. For two consecutive years, this mysterious black-masked character has been the UDW champion. He has never ever lost a match in his life! Before agreeing to defend his title, he insists on being paid an obscenely high sum of money. Each time, his price is higher than before. Being interviewed, he comes across as an arrogant and conceited comic book character. In the ring, he's totally unstable and impossible to control.

He does anything and everything to win . . . scratching eyeballs, biting arms—and that's only for starters! Apparently in the past he has killed opponents in the squared circle. Not tonight. During this eerie event, he just maims the hell out of a poor fool who calls himself: CRUD THE STUD. If the whole mess wasn't so absolutely unbelievable, MONEY-SPINNER would scare me silly! The really scary part is finding out that MONEY-SPINNER is a crowd favourite.

Explosions galore are happening all around me. Voices resound with approval and disapproval over the way a particular fight is going, of the refereeing or lack thereof, or about the announcers and those lame interviews with wrestlers. My fellow Fissurites, mostly the guys, are jumping up and down, while their girlfriends sit and giggle. Wow. I have to admit, I'm not impressed one bit.

AS HALLOWEEN NIGHT FLICKERS ALONG the girls take over the kitchen to do their gossiping stuff (may sound sexist but happens to be true in this case).

Meanwhile I follow the rest of the guys as they lumber their way down below and into the basement. Even with lights on, it's dark down here and this is the only room in Cynthia's house I haven't seen before. There's a dusty cement floor, a couple of beat-up old sofas, lots of boxes piled up all over the place, a musty smell you'd expect from cellars. And nothing's painted white—or any other colour.

As I drink from my third beer, I listen in on the guys talking.

"FRATS is goin' nowhere," says a short bulldog guy with black steel-wool hair. "Nobody wants the same old crap anymore."

Somebody else insists, "We hav'ta add to the roster."

They all begin throwing in their two cents worth, speaking at the same time and over each other. The tension grows. Testosterone can be so tiresome.

"Well maybe if we didn't have everybody wantin' to win all the time."

"Screw you! You're useless!"

"What? Hey, how 'bout last week?"

"Ah, give it up! You were lucky."

"We gotta have somethin' that's way out crazy . . ."

"Lucky, eh? Come on, right now, let's go!"

"More extreme is the only way that FRATS can . . ."

"Tables and boards? Everybody's doin' tables and boards, gimme a break . . ."

"All right, I'm down with that! Be prepared to die!"

This final remark causes us all to clam up and follow these two bigmouths as they move into another room. I'm expecting them to slug it out and get it over with, whatever their dispute is. An unusual thing happens. This is no ordinary basement.

We are now in a larger open area where the two guys are standing and glaring evil-eyed at each other. I look around and see a couple of bed mattresses, side by side, and there are even a few rows of chairs—an audience section. Part of the herd, I sit with the others and watch. Dan emerges, holding a camcorder to film it all.

These guys start to put on a little pro-wrestling type show. It brings back memories of the bonfire. Obviously everything's in good fun. They even laugh while messing up some moves. Sometimes there's a pause in the play. That's when they whisper to each other what they plan to do next. This action is more riveting than what I've just seen on TV, which isn't saying a whole lot.

Time travels on and many of the girls (including mine) come down to be entertained by some primitive male exertion. Cynthia fills me in that this impromptu practice, breaking out every now and then, is part of FRATS, an acronym for 'Fissure Rock All-Teen Sports.' It's the local backyard wrestling federation. I guess they weren't able to find a way to fit into their name the letter 'W' for Wrestling. Since the weather has taken a turn for the colder, they are basement wrestling now until the warmer spring weather returns.

The spontaneous match has finally fizzled to an unremarkable end, and discussions linger over what to keep in the "real show" and what should be added that wasn't there to begin with, and so on.

Out of the blue Dan yells, "I want Jim!"

My immediate reaction is to chortle, 'Whoa there, little buddy, I'm already taken. Remember, by your sister?' Saying nothing, I wait and wonder where this is headed.

One of the other guys isn't so sure. "Dan, this new guy's gotta learn moves . . . you know the rules."

Cynthia's brother marches to the centre of the open space and strikes up a challenging pose that I don't like. He looks at me, and I feel cornered or something. "Come on, Jim. Just wanna show ya some moves. Nothin' that'll hurt, promise."

This is all so childish. I don't want a repeat of that Full Nelson episode.

The other guy says, "Go easy on him, bro." Damn, he's just given Dan the green light.

I look to Cynthia for a way out.

She holds the camcorder that Dan has just handed her. "You don't mind, do you, Jim?" She might as well have just shot me. She knows I can't deny her anything.

Christ, to hell with my reservations . . . whatever. I walk out onto the make-believe ring, stepping boldly into strange new territory. Standing as I am on these old bed mattresses, I guess you could say I'm expanding my comfort zone.

Dan begins by showing me an arm-bar. Later he explains how I must spring back from the invisible ropes, where he pushes me, to take a clothesline and fall down hard. He pegs me with the nickname "JimmyJobber." That means my job as a jobber is simple: take everything that's dished out to me and lose to him at the end. I'm not supposed to fight back, unless he tells me to, ahead of time, and that will only happen if he figures it'll make the match less boring to watch.

Basically it's no big deal. We begin. I shrug my way through it, understanding my role.

Things change fast when we are facing each other and he puts one arm over my shoulder, and slips his other arm right under my crotch. That's far too close to my manhood for comfort. I step to the side quickly, avoiding the follow-through. "Hey, what're you doing?" I demand.

"Body-slam, man!" he answers with characteristic determined fire in his eyes.

"Forget it," I say. Hey, it's not like wimping out. I'm just thinking why should I let Dan control the whole show? At this moment I am very aware of Cynthia filming us and of the other guys watching. Am I simply going to walk through this match and get beaten by a fourteen-year-old? I don't think so. "Come here!" I yell, assuming a more assertive role for my character and for myself—I've got to be more proactive!

"Ah!" he shouts out, as I grab him in a side headlock. I even pretend to pummel away at his trapped head with my free fist. Then I flip him over and land on top of him. He struggles to regain the advantage, only I'm not going to let that happen.

The crowd around us is getting louder. I am showing a new side of myself to them and they're receptive to it. The new guy can wrestle. I've got respect going on here. Fair enough, my opponent is Cynthia's little brother; still I seem to be a natural at this anyway. I'm even surprising myself.

Dan is unhappy with my innovations. "You stupid shit! When I get outta this, you're fuckin' dead!" he screams. Hmm, the way Dan expresses anger sure dips low into his vocabulary. Swearing does seem to suit his personality, though.

Once we've scrambled to our feet Dan tries for the same scoop as he had seconds before and I prevent it again, this time by dropping to my knees and clasping his calves, pulling forward so he lands on his back. Sensing my timing to be right, I go for the cover. I hear the guys counting, "One, two—"

My head hurts. I roll onto my back and look up at Joe, who's holding a plastic baseball bat. The first phrase that enters my mind is, 'Boy, can those toy bats ever sting like hell.'

"Next week, JimmyJobber!" Joe proclaims. "You and me'll be in the squared circle, and I'll teach you what your job really is!"

Well, everyone cracks up over that one.

Dan's the exception. "You asshole!" He gets up, grabs the bat and starts chasing Joe.

They run around the basement, and Cynthia aims the camcorder at the two new combatants.

My head continues to throb. No way will I complain. I take my bumps and bruises like a man.

Joe is laughing wildly, higher than an airplane.

Dan's fuming for real. And he's swinging that hard plastic bat around dangerously, slightly missing Joe's head several times as they both wind back and forth through the spectators. Dan gripes, "I would've kicked out myself if it wasn't for you, fucknut!" Yup, he sure takes his wrestling seriously.

This continues until Cynthia lowers the camcorder and announces that the battery has run out. Hopefully she'll be able to delete some of her brother's profanity when she edits the video. Dan keeps grumbling about how he would have beaten me easily.

I get to my feet—no easy feat—and get a few slaps on the back from a number of the guys. Mild congratulations.

"You look like you belong in the ring there, Jim."

"Yeah, not bad."

What do you say? I say thanks, feeling my confidence level on the rise.

I'M ALONE WITH CYNTHIA on her porch, and there's silence between us. It doesn't feel so cold out anymore as I look into her bluer than blue eyes and we communicate without saying a word, without touching. I'm not suggesting we're reading each other's minds exactly, but I'm sure we're musing over a similar script in our brains.

Searching through her eyes, I know precisely what I'm saying to her. 'Cynthia, I wish we were both adults with no parents to get in our way. We'd go back to my apartment and I could prove my love to you. Since day one at school when I first saw you, I had to have you. We need to be together.'

I know she shares the conversation I'm having inside my sore head. We kiss and hold onto each other and I can taste the flavour of her Halloween lipstick as it smudges all over my face. We understand the reality of our situation, however, as I get ready to walk home. My parents are waiting and her mother will soon be making her reappearance. We're trapped, like Romeo and Juliet (well, sort of). Parting—such sweet sorrow.

From the sidewalk, I look back at her in that tempting black dress. Beside her, fading away in orange embers, are the contorted smiles of those jack-o-lanterns on the railing.

ROCK TWELVE

HERE WE GO. It's Saturday, and I'm at 7 Shroud Circle again. Of course it marks my final visit to this house, at least with Andy living there. During our swimming and diving in his pool, we say nothing meaningful. His invitation surprised me because I thought he said he wanted a low-profile departure—the subject hasn't come up.

Seven days have slipped by since that successful Halloween bash at Cynthia's. Now I'm officially on the FRATS roster; my first match against Joe starts tonight. We've talked a couple of times in school about it. We'll do a bit of general planning right before our event. That way, we agreed, it will look unrehearsed when we start filming. Should be fun I think.

Naturally I don't tell any of this to Andy, especially on his last afternoon in town. His parents and the movers are already at work elsewhere in the gigantic house, so there's no point in asking him the questions I remain really curious about—such as what's up with this silent rift between him and the other kids at FRH? It will all be history before this day is done, so there.

I've just finished jumping into the water and as I swim towards the ledge, he asks me in a clear calm tone, "Ever consider killing yourself?"

When I look up at him, there's not a trace of emotion on his face. "My dive was that bad?"

He keeps on, "Seriously."

God, I hate talking about things like death, you know? "Never," I answer, making sure he hears the certainty in my voice.

"You'd rather grow old and die, all shrunken up like a prune?"

Pulling myself onto the deck, I gain foot balance and give him a slight push on his upper arm. "Maybe it's not so bad." I march toward the diving board, but his selected topic for discussion isn't going to splash away so easily.

"Think about how quick and simple it would be, and painless." Sunbeams streaming through one of the ceiling windows strike his strangely smiling face. It's almost as though he's daydreaming, far away, unaware that I am with him. He looks so relaxed. Weird.

"Earth to Andy," I try to snip off this quiet spell he's got himself under, and I stop my procession to the board in deference to my friend. "Dive, man. And don't go off the deep end on me, huh?" I cough, embarrassed by my unfunny joke. He appears all right again with an okay drop into the water, except he stays down for longer than I appreciate.

Finally, breaking back to the surface, Andy yells, "Hey!" His brown eyes are open wide as his arms tread effortlessly. "They say drowning is the most peaceful way to go."

"Who were they, when they last spoke to you, guy?" I say under my breath.

"What?"

Then I think of something better. "The water'll wrinkle you up like a prune before you actually die. You wouldn't want that, right?" I'm trying my best to dissuade him from these wayward thoughts without being totally obvious.

Andy, still treading, studies me absent-mindedly as I stand on the ledge. "Yeah." And his voice quietly bounces off the walls.

WHAT CAN I SAY about Mr. and Mrs. Bradford? After my friend and I finish our swim and have used separate change rooms to get into our regular clothes, we bump into his folks in the front foyer that is way too large for any family. I've never set eyes on either one of them until now, and they don't even offer me a greeting. Talk about rude.

First off, they're old. I swear they must be in their sixties, and they've got a sixteen-year-old kid? I'm not saying there's anything wrong with that. It's just unusual. Andy's old man is bald and wearing a formal grey suit with a tie, like he's off to work. This is their moving day! His mother's not much different in her flowery dress that ladies probably wear to tea parties and stuff. Both of them have sagging permanent-looking frowns on their faces. They're directing the movers precisely where to put boxes on the truck. The trouble is they are arguing even with one another over where things should go.

She speaks in a kind of high-class English accent, "No, no, Ronald. The fine china must be kept away from anything that might cause it to chip."

He is just as frightfully British. "But my dear, everything is packaged safely enough inside each box."

"We cannot be too careful. Each piece is priceless; moreover, there's a sentimental value attached."

The old man looks at Andy and me, finally acknowledging we exist. His tone is sharp, unfriendly, "What does Andrew's young friend think?" He eyes me up and down like a hawk.

I'm thinking it's a bizarre question to be asking. Neither Andy nor I say anything.

"Oh, Ronald, really!" Mrs. Bradford admonishes her husband. "Any associate of Andrew's would most certainly know nothing regarding anything!" She goes on to give her only child an ugly, scornful glance.

I can't figure this out at all, and I'm feeling really uneasy being here with these two disagreeable ancient people.

The movers are getting restless. "Folks, we do have a schedule to keep."

"Now listen here," Mr. Bradford begins in a rattled way, "I'm not in the habit of being rushed! May I remind you that you are being paid a handsome sum of money?" Then, while still talking to the mover guy, it's father's turn to pick on Andy. "Why, you're practically as incompetent as this son of mine!" And the thick chunk of hatred in Bradford Senior's voice makes me want to land my fist flat in his face for dissing my pal.

Mrs. Bradford pipes in with an I-told-you-so, "I still say Chasen Van Lines would have been much more professional."

Andy's face is a mixture of boredom and shame. His parents continue their way with the movers for longer than I can stick around to listen. I've got other stuff planned.

"Well," I extend my hand, "see you later. Remember, stay out of that deep end, buddy."

"Don't worry. The new place doesn't have a pool." He shakes my hand and slips a piece of paper into it. "Call, or write me sometime . . . if you want." His soft words sound thin, tired, monotonous.

I look at what he's given me: phone number, snail and e-mail addresses. "Cool."

"Bye," he says.

"Bye." I walk away, kind of sad.

One thing I'll tell you for sure. I would not trade parents with my departing friend for all the money in the world. No way. If they're like that all the time—poor Andy.

WE WANT DINNER. First, we must wait for Lisa to come down from her room where she's all tangled up in the world-wide web. Could take a while.

Dad says to Mom, "I think she's just bored. Maybe once she discovers boys—"

"That's what I'm afraid of!" Mom stops him. She's rushing around, putting a few final things onto the table. "I have a pretty good inkling about the sordid type of people who frequent those chat lines, the things that go on. It's on the news practically every night. I still say we should get rid of it altogether."

Dad makes a smiley face. "Honey, times are changing. We can't go back to when we were young. It's not the same now. Right, Jim?"

Oh, I knew he'd do this to me. I maintain my neutrality, "I dunno." Really, how the hell am I supposed to know? Sometimes Dad thinks I'm his age.

Lisa comes bounding down the stairs. "I'm here." She sits down, and starts munching away at the salad like a big rabbit with an avaricious appetite.

To say my sister is cheerful would be overkill. Interestingly I've noticed lately, whenever Dad's home, her bitchiness gauge does read low.

She says to me, "So is Jimbo off to Cynthia-land tonight?" Sure that teasing tone's there, but nothing outwardly offensive. Lisa then takes huge gulps from her glass of milk and piles the roast beef onto her plate. There's nothing anorexic about her.

"You guessed right, Leese," I finally answer.

As I look at her less-than-confrontational face, I can see the reason for her mood change is not simply because Dad's home. Something happened on the chat line. Has she found someone new? Maybe she and Gerald have reconnected. He's the same age as Lisa and (back in the city) more than once, when I came home and my parents weren't in, I caught the two of them 'frolicking.' I did nothing. All it amounted to was one step beyond puppy love. The day before we moved up here they broke up, and I made a promise to my sister that I would never mention her involvement with Gerald to anyone. I'm not sure why this is such a big deal to Lisa, but she doesn't want Mom or Dad to find out they were ever together. No matter what, I keep my promises.

In a way I can relate to my sister about this. I mean Cynthia and I have been closer with each other than Gerald and Lisa ever were, and I don't want my parents to know either. It wouldn't be right. At the same time, I'm getting impatient. Exactly when are Cynthia and I going to . . . do it? Should I press the issue, or just wait for her to show me a sign? Maybe it's a guy thing with me, macho pride? I'm a big bag of mixed feelings.

Dad chips in, "Seeing a lot of Sally's daughter, aren't you?" I'm not sure if there's a message there or not. Regardless, I treat his question as rhetorical.

Mom finds it hard to realize her little boy is growing up. "I want you back in this house before midnight. Understand?"

I nod. We all know what happened to Cinderella, don't we?

SMOKIN' MAN IS THE WRESTLING CHARACTER name

Joe has chosen for himself. Suitable? You bet. While we prepare in Cynthia's basement for our event, he's already got a joint lit up. He has the look of a messed-up kind of guy. Black leather jacket with chains looped on both sides, a real biker-type wardrobe. If I didn't know him, I don't think I'd want to. Guess that goes to show how you should never judge by appearances because he's an okay guy. A bit of a skid, rough around the edges, but hey, even I have faults—plenty of them.

Dan was the one who opened the front door tonight. He explained to me that his sis' would be down soon, although that was half an hour ago. She's got a migraine. In the meantime her little bro is the one who's getting ready to film this match.

Joe walks closer to me, offers me a toke.

I take a few drags to be sociable, then wipe my lips with a tissue from my jeans pocket.

"Okay, Jim, how's about you start off with a s'prise attack? Like somethin' nobody'd expect from JimmyJobber?"

"'K."

"When I give you my forearm smash, that's your signal I'm taking over, and I'll keep quashin' you till the final pin. I won't hurt you or nothin'."

I'm glad he inserted that last assurance. I don't want a repeat of the plastic baseball bat over my head.

Dan shouts, "Let's get it on!" The word hyper is way too mellow to describe this kid as he's all pumped to film us. "Our first match," he imitates a professional announcer as the camcorder microphone tapes his breaking voice, "is gonna be starting any minute now. Here comes Smokin' Man!"

Walking in front of the camera, Joe puts on an evil scowl. His words are spoken in a raspy whisper, a deep dark taunting tone. "JimmyJobber is gonna be trained by the Smokin' Man tonight, in front of everyone's eyes, for sure." He trudges his way to the mattresses.

"Woooooh," Dan responds in a clownish way, "I don't know about you folks at home, but I'm pretty scared. Let's get JimmyJobber out here." He aims the camera at me. "Anything worth saying, there, Jobber?"

A bit on the spot and in the bright light, I think of something quickly. "You're in for a surprise, Mr. Announcer guy." I put my face closer to the camera lens and scream, "You're all in for a surprise!" Moving to the ring area where Joe awaits me, I'm worrying about Cynthia. Migraine? Is she in bed? I can picture her in my head. Should I go see if she's all right?

Laughter from Dan. "Yeah, okay, whatever. We all know a jobber can jabber. Let's see how he wrestles. Ding-ding!"

Joe and I circle around on top of the mattresses and stare at each other.

I know I'm supposed to make the first few moves, and I'm trying to think of a good start. "What's that?" I point behind him.

He turns his head, and I swing my right leg around to lightly kick at his knees from behind. Immediately Joe's on his back.

Dan: "Okay, gotta hand it to him. This new jobber just got Smokin' Man with the oldest trick in the book. But how long can he keep the momentum goin'?"

I deliver a damn good elbow drop to Joe's chest, making sure it hardly connects. He does a great sell by thrashing about and gagging, making it look like I nailed him straight on the old Adam's apple.

I grab him by his hair and lead him to his feet, then wallop him a few times to the back of the head. Joe plays that to the hilt as well. Hey, I'm really starting to like this.

Next I push him into the invisible ropes. When he rushes back toward the centre of our so-called ring, I clothesline him and he is flat on his back again.

Dan: "Boring match so far. Jobber's got no power moves at all, just goin' through the motions."

(Christ, Cynthia's little brother is annoying as hell.)

Joe leaps to his feet, a nip-up, and I see the forearm smash coming to the top of my head. I brace for it, although it doesn't actually hurt. Still I thud to my knees and moan as if I've got a concussion or something. He follows up with a few stomps on my back, and eventually I go limp and flatten out onto my stomach.

Dan: "Looks like Jobber's had his fifteen seconds of fame, folks! We all know once Smokin' Man gets lit up, there's no putting him out."

Now I have no choice but to take exactly what is thrown at me. This was the agreement. I'm a man of my words.

Somebody's got to be pulling my hair, I feel, as Joe guides me to my feet. This time he pushes me to the ropes, and when I bounce back he gives me some sort of judo chop to the gut. I sell this big-time, doing a somersault in mid-air, landing hard on my arse.

Dan: "That was sick! This is gettin' way better now."

Joe stands me up again and prepares his next move. I'm bent over facing the mattresses and he is in front of me, locking his arms around my waist, his torso flush with my back. Suddenly Joe lifts me up, holding me in the air upside-down. I'm propped up, sitting on his shoulders, facing behind him.

Dan: "YEAH! Here it comes!"

Down I go with a thump, on my back.

Dan: "Powerbomb! Nicely executed!"

That kind of winded me.

Joe, sensing I need some time to catch my breath back, walks closer to the camera. "Ya see," he says in a muffled voice, "I could pin this nobody here and now, but I wanna have my fun first."

When I stand up, thinking I'm ready to go on, Cynthia comes down the stairs and I turn to glance at her. Joe grabs me from behind, raises me, and drives me downwards. The bottom of my spine jams hard against his knee. We actually did rehearse this move a few times before and, if I'd been paying attention, I would have cushioned the impact by getting my feet down first. I was distracted, though, I wasn't ready for it, and it ends up really smarting.

"OW!" I yelp, and I curl up into a ball on the mattresses. Not only does my tailbone hurt, but also a part of my, uh, private parts made contact during that last manoeuvre. So I'm seeing stars and all that sort of thing.

Dan: "An awesome atomic drop! Guess who's not havin' kids, folks?" He laughs while I hurt.

Cynthia does nothing, as I am able to sneak a glimpse of her from my helpless foetal position. She is sitting on one of the steps looking at me with nothing on her face to tell me what she's thinking or how she's feeling, like a beautiful bird that won't chirp.

By the time I make it back up to my hands and knees, Joe bends down. He whispers in my ear, "Y'okay?"

I cough. I suppose I am as I mutter, "Yeah."

After all this, Joe takes it easy on me for the next few minutes. I'm assaulted with clotheslines, numerous punches to my head and shoulders. They're perfectly harmless of course; all of them I do pretend jobs on. I'm beginning to feel all right again, until he decides to go for his finisher.

It begins with the same move Dan tried last week. Joe faces me, slides one arm over my shoulder and his other arm scoops me up between my legs—not too comfortable, let me tell you.

Dan: "Yeah, he's goin' for it! Do it, Smokin' Man!"

So I'm up in the air, sideways. Then I tumble down as he directs my back onto his knee. This is painful, but not as bad as what went on a few moments before. Again I sell it with a big, "Awgh!" He finally goes for the pin.

Dan does the count: "1-2-3! JimmyJobber, useless as a jobber can be. Your winner, no contest, Smokin' Man!"

To celebrate the victory (I guess it's his trademark), he lights up another joint. Joe blows the smoke into the camera. "Don't-cha all wish you were me?"

He walks off and sits down on a couch behind the camera. "Good job, Jim," he tells me. "Looks like you're prime for workin' in front of an audience." His eyes are half-shut and glazed.

Hooray for me, I tell myself sarcastically. My back aches, and as I lie there on the mattresses, Dan does a camcorder close-up of my agonized face. I've got bad feelings running through me. It's my historical emotions grating at me from inside—back to when I was eight, being degraded by that former friend in my old neighbourhood.

Despite this I stand up, smile at Cynthia, and wave. She returns my gesture without smiling. I wonder what's wrong, and I'm going to find out.

LATER, IN HER ROOM, she fesses up after I pester her a bit. "My migraine's gone, thank goodness. Sometimes I think I take on too much at school."

I'm glad she's feeling better (my own body is bent out of shape). "Can't you drop some of the hundreds of things you do for the school?"

She smiles and looks at me with twinkling eyes. "Oh, I know what you want?"

"What's that?" I ask, genuinely unknowing. I sense some slight alarm inside myself, like I'm going to be put into another wrestling hold.

She walks over to where I'm sitting on her bed. "You want me all to yourself."

I swallow hard. That's not exactly what I meant, but can you blame me if I'm not going to argue? Funny how I coil a little as she puts her arms around me. No kidding, I want her bad. Still I'm nervous, if that makes any sense.

Cynthia mistakes my reluctance for pain and gets all motherly, "Oh, Jim, poor guy. Joe really did a number on you, didn't he? Here, lie down on your stomach."

Fine, I do precisely as I'm told. The pink quilt on top of her bed smells like red rose perfume, like her.

She begins by massaging those muscles that attach your neck to your shoulders. "This is where tension gets all tied up, right in here. Just feel it and relax." I don't fight at all as she removes my sweater. "So much better," she says. "Skin against skin."

Oh boy, I'm mostly relaxed, except, to tell the truth, part of me is . . . stiff. Telling more of the truth, I felt this same way that afternoon when we were alone on the dock and she had caressed my bare leg with hers. I must say something to her now, no matter how weak. "Feels good." I don't know what else to say; words won't work.

My entire back is being expertly massaged now. Cynthia leaves me momentarily to get some baby oil and rubs that in, too. She lies down on top of me and kisses the nape of my neck, then licks me there again and again with the tip of her tender tongue. I've got these incredible shivers running up my spine and I'm thinking how much better all this is than wrestling with Joe!

I turn over so I can face her as she remains on top of me. We can't control ourselves any longer. We embrace and kiss and make all sorts of making out sounds, just like in the movies! This is so new to me, and somehow I'm just letting nature take its course. God bless Mother Nature, I tell myself!

Suddenly, the door swings open and in pops Sally Sacalla's drunken little head. "Oops, sorry kids! Guess what? I'm home. G'night."

The door closes at the same time as my inflated expectations, among other things, quickly deflate. Good night is right.

ROCK THIRTEEN

YOU CAN'T PROPERLY ENJOY city snow. Up here in Fissure Rock, fluffy flakes covering evergreens, leafless trees and grassy fields make quite the breathtaking sight. Everywhere you turn looks like a postcard or a famous nature painting. It's now late in November, and the white stuff has come to stay. This is the news I learn from Cynthia. She tells me not to expect it to start melting until mid-April. Whenever I walk around town, cold clear crisp air makes me feel alive and clean. Thick snow layers act as buffers, absorbing sharp sounds, from people shouting, to car doors slamming nearby, to trains clanking along and whistling far off on the other side of the highway. It really is a walk through a beautiful dream.

Certain things have happened in the past few weeks, new and not so new stuff. My schoolwork's the same old thing: in English, I get 90s. Of course, all you have to do is show up for Gym and you're rewarded with a 60; I do better than that which explains my 75. But I've had to work hard at Math and Science for those bare passes (51 and 54). This isn't likely to change much by the time first report cards come out next week, so there shouldn't be any surprises. As for FRATS, I've had a few more matches where I've jobbed for some bigger guys. I accept a few minor injuries, nothing spectacular. It makes Cynthia happy because Dan loves to film it all, which keeps him out of her hair.

Speaking of Cynthia, we've had a few more of what I call our 'sessions.' I don't want to be a kiss-and-tell (I can't stand those guys who are), so let's just say we're familiar with third base. Basically both she and I are not ready to go all the way. I'm inexperienced and I'm sure she is, too. Probably someday Cynthia and I will do the whole she-bang, only no time soon. We let our school friends think whatever they want.

That's another thing. With Andy gone, I'm getting along great with the other kids. Don't get me wrong, Andy was a good friend and I miss him. At the same time it's kind of like he stood in the way of me making the good acquaintances I now enjoy. The past belongs to history; no sense holding onto stuff gone bye-bye. All things put together, I have to say my life is cruising along just fine.

Cynthia has plunged into organizing events at school to raise funds for the new library and the swimming pool. Chocolate sales are still in progress, well ahead of last year at this time. The slave auction went off without a hitch, and was too funny. You'll have to use your imagination for that one. What's still to come includes a talent show, where students who are into acting and singing can strut their stuff in hopes of applause. It should also do okay. I didn't and won't get involved in any of these things (I'm way too shy), and I'm stubbornly wondering about something else.

Fissure Rock is not a rich town. How is Cynthia going to reach her ambitious fundraising goals with these little patchwork type activities? Although I'm lousy at math, I can add two and two together. They continue to equal four and nothing more.

FRIDAY NIGHT. Being the middle-age romantics they are, Mom and Dad have gone to see a movie. I'm sitting on my bed finger-picking guitar chords, searching for the right ones to go with, while taking stock of how great everything in this wee spot of the universe is unfolding. Even more snow is falling gently outside my window. I remember, back home, Sideline used to lie down beside me and purr while we both watched the flakes fall. Sounds sucky, but I miss that darn cat.

Now I don't know what coaxes me, whether it's a combination of thoughts about Andy and Cynthia and Sideline and the snow out there, but I grab a pen and start writing lyrics to the soft music that has drifted into my head from nowhere. Feeling detached, I begin floating helplessly halfway between the mythical moon and mother Earth. Even though I'm okay with my life at this specific joint in time, I write down these lonely heart-wounded words.

> You are the cloud that hides the sun
> I know that I'm no one, but even then
> Why can't I touch you, shadow friend?
>
> Trapped in these shades of hell today
> I know you'll never go my way, but I pretend
> That I am with you, shadow friend
>
> My eyes are open wide
> But darkness pours inside
> Shadow friend, shadow friend
>
> Dreaming of maybe, if, possibly
> I know I'm thinking of me, but still I send
> All my love to shadow friend

Next I decide to go all the way and sing it through while playing. Immersed in a deep melancholic trance, I shut my eyes and picture the audience out there in the dark concert hall (thousands of them) quietly listening to me, raising burning lighters above their heads, sharing my soulful experience. I finish the performance perfectly, but the applause is interrupted by reality.

A swift swoosh and my door is open. "Jimmy? You better see this." Lisa's worried.

Returning my guitar to the corner, I follow my sister into her bedroom, trying to guess what kind of trouble she's got herself into.

She points at her computer screen, like any second it'll start shooting out out radioactive sparks. The computer was actually given to both of us by Mom and Dad, and I have to forever fight with her to use it for typing my school essays.

I look at the website causing her so much distress. The bright red-and-yellow font bellows out: 'BACKYARD BOYS!' Figuring it's porn, I'm not sure what made her think I'd be interested in this. "Leese, what's up your sleeve?"

"Just scroll down those letters," she demands.

Sitting down, I decide to please her. All right, I soon unravel that this is a page full of different backyard wrestling 'federations,' mostly from all over North America. I must admit to being guardedly interested, and I start with the letter 'A.' In front of me is 'Adam and Eve Wrestling.' Clicking on the name, I'm sent to a picture gallery revealing a sparsely attired supposedly married couple, claiming to be the genuine originators of backyard wrestling. Their 'sons', ranging in age from 11 to 19, are also shown. There are photos of these guys wrestling with each other and with friends—all are dressed in loincloths. I don't see the big deal, really. It's weird, sure, but that's the world these days.

Lisa commands me, "Get back to the main page and go down to F."

Past my eyes fly all the B, C, D and E feds. A few names down the F list and my right hand jumps off the mouse. There it is, 'Fissure Rock All-Teen Sports (FRATS) Backyard Wrestling'. Kind of strange to see the small group of guys I wrestle with immediately available to a whole world of internet users. I grab the mouse again and click on the large graphic on the screen. Now I'm given a choice of where to go next: History, Roster, Events, Photos, Videos for Sale, Message Board, E-mail.

Lisa doesn't have to say anything further; I feel her frightened breathing over my shoulder as I navigate my way through the site options. My curiosity has been piqued. Foregoing History, I quickly view the Roster. I notice: KILLER DAN, SMOKIN' MAN, several others, and . . . JIMMYJOBBER. I open the icon of the one last mentioned.

My own face is on the screen, all scrunched up in a sleeper hold, staring back at me in anguish. Below my picture is the caption: 'JIMMYJOBBER, 5'8, 145 pounds.' A commentary follows: 'Has never won a match, but gives it his all, which ends up being a pathetic loss every time out. The biggest loser ever to dwell on Ducksback Drive . . . waddling nowhere, fast.'

My next destination is Videos. As expected, some of my matches are among those being offered on a generous selection of 6-hour compilations (at $50 per crack). I'm not too down with that, or how I'm finding out about all this (by complete surprise). But I don't see any reason to panic. "How did you even find this site anyway?"

"What does it matter?" She frantically goes through a quick explanation. "Look, I heard about FRATS at my school. It's really hype there and this girl I know, Katy, she really likes Danny Sacalla, but she only gets to see him at recess because he's in Special Ed." She stumbles, stops her explanation. "Anyway she gave me the website address and told me I should check it out. There! Are you satisfied?"

Because I've never seen her this way before, I have to ask the question, "Leese, what is here that's got you so bugged out?"

Sounding like she's giving me directions to Dracula's castle, she says, "Go to the Message Board."

I have to tell the absolute truth. There's something in her voice that makes me not want to go there.

Following many seconds of hesitation, I click on the link which delivers the Message Board to my eyes. Several lines of writing appear. Judging by the dates attached to them, this page attracts about three visitors daily, at least those who feel the need to write some sort of statement . . .

> *Dec. 5:* Awesome graphics, but your wrestlers couldn't beat ours on a cold day in hell. We're just 10 miles north of you, if you have the balls.
>
> -Julian from Shift Creek Wrestling

> *Dec. 5:* Hey, you know me, in Topeka, Kansas. I want to buy another tape of FRATS Wrestling. Do you still do the custom-made ones, cuz I want to see Killer Dan beat Smokin Man

by puttin him through a board, so let me know and I'll pay the bucks—you remember me, I'm good for it.
               -Bob, no fed

Dec. 5: You need more wrestlers, but if you want to trade tapes with us, we'll do that. Our stuff's mostly in French. We're in Montreal. Check out our website.
            -Stephane, Wham-Slam Wrestling

Dec. 4: JimmyJobber, you sure are CUTE! I really like you, lots! Love watching you get tossed around . . . very sexy . . . I'd pay to see MORE of you. C'mon, everybody's got a price! I'm at close quarters, boy!
              -Mr. Kween, a BIG fan

That final December 4th entry has shaken up every cell in my body. I pore over it repeatedly. Each word cuts sharply into me. Finally I can read no further. This is impossible. Some guy out there likes me in . . . that way? God, I'm going to throw up!

"Jimmy?" Lisa whispers from another world. "What are you going to do?"

"Um." Good question. My thoughts are running around like squirrels in my head. First of all, who put the page up? Cynthia would not do this. She didn't know what was on the message board, or she would have had this indecent entry deleted by now. Or maybe it's Dan's page? Possibly, but he's not the brightest bulb in the box. Could he set up something looking this professional on his own? Or Joe? Not likely.

My sister tells me, "Anyone can find the street we live on. Your picture's on the roster, too. Wherever this man is who calls himself Mr. Kween, he could be looking for you! Jimmy, you know what I'm afraid of, don't you?"

I turn to look at her, and she's close to crying. We've both been transported into a bizarre horror flick. No, this can't be happening. "Stop it!" I shout, alarming even myself. Then I do my best to calm down, clear my throat, "Somebody's playing a lousy joke. I'll talk to Cynthia and get it all smoothed out."

My feet promptly propel me from her room. Gingerly my hand shuts my bedroom door and I begin pacing the floor. Breathing fast and shallow, I feel light-headed. Just when you think things are going your way . . .

ROCK FOURTEEN

I'M ON COFFEE NUMBER TWO, and I don't even like the stuff, as I sit on the chilly wooden chair inside Lynda's Home Cooking. They're out of hot chocolate, but I need something to warm up my bones. Nothing has changed in this place. It's another early Saturday morning with the regular crew presiding. That Renaldo character has got his massive elbows on the counter. He seems to be frozen in time: no younger of course, no older either. I come here when I have some heavy thinking to do, so it's been a while. And I know that my fellow FRHers never pop in, which suits me.

A ghostly early morning fog blocks the sunrays trying to slip through the frosted window at the side of my head. What do I do? This new twist of fate in my life at Fissure Rock is way beyond anything that happened back in the city. I decide not to go there. No, once I entered high school and met Bryan, Mason and Wendy, I promised myself to leave that bad memory behind. So I allow the charming conversation between Lynda and Renaldo to fill the troubled space between my ears.

"I tell ya, Lynn, I'm gettin' real sick of havin' to drive down to that goddamn hole ever' week!" The bass of his voice practically rattles the loose wooden panels on the wall.

Lynda tries cheering him up some while she fries her popular scrambled eggs. "Come on, that's why they pay you the big bucks, darlin'! It's only one day a week. And watch your language. We got a minor in here." Lynda winks at me, making sure I know she's simply ribbing Renaldo.

The big guy gives me a strange quick glance, like a sudden bolt of lightning I wasn't expecting. I'm waiting for a roar of thunder to follow. Instead, he turns his head away, puffs greedily on the cigarette stuck between his fingers and blows out with a deep disgusted sigh, "Kids."

Definitely my signal to leave. I'm not hanging around this place with a miserable old fart who's on a rant. His whole face reads regret, failure, anger and just generally antagonistic feelings. Hey, I don't need his problems. Got my own. With payment and tip on table, I get up and go.

Ten-thirty. While I trudge towards no place special, snow crunches under my boots. It makes me feel heavy and forceful above it. Cold air is snapping my mind back into proper position. I've got to find out more about the website message board deal, even though I feel like I've already got too much information. My winter-visible breath makes me feel stronger and my pace quickens. No more hedging. I vow to face this mess right on.

CYNTHIA ISN'T HOME. Dan and Joe answer the door, both dressed only in shorts and streaming with sweat. They're somewhere past stoned. I'm invited in.

"We been pumpin' iron," says Dan in a puppy dog way, closing the door after me.

"Where's your sister?" I reply.

Thoroughly enjoying his high, Dan starts laughing.

Joe answers, "Library." He continues to huff and puff. "Research."

Dan tries to talk me into staying when he sees me put on my hat again. "Joe and me got some new moves we're workin' on. Be awesome if ya could practice with us. FRATS is gonna kick ass and be the best backyard fed anywhere, man!"

"Yeah?" Time to reveal what I know. "I suppose you're going to tape the episode where Mr. Kween pays me a visit? That'll sell a truckload of videos, won't it?"

Joe's first to respond. "Uh, what are you talkin' bout?"

"You see, Joe, I can't figure out if you're clueless because your brain cells are so totally wiped away, or if you're just lying!" Although I'm rolling along my line of hostility, I am also holding my breath. Joe's bigger than me, and I'm not exactly sure what he's capable of doing.

Looking down at his toes, Dan speaks next and he sounds serious enough. "Jim? Joe doesn't know. But it 'aint that bad. I mean that guy's prob'ly nothin' but an old geezer havin' some lame kind-a fun."

I give him a stone cold stare. "I'm out of FRATS!"

I'm out of patience.

And I'm out the door.

CYNTHIA'S NOT AT THE LIBRARY. No surprise. My mother's there. She has to work every fourth Saturday in addition to weekdays. We've never been in this place together, mother and son. Mom smiles as soon as I walk in. Isn't that sweet? I hang around until her lunch break. My feet wander around the aisles of shelves and my eyes zigzag the titles of books. Bleakly I ponder how many of the people who wrote these are now dead. I switch gears and spin a more positive outlook around in my head. For one thing, it's a relief to be getting some quiet and warmth. There are no hassles in here and no smoking. Maybe I'll start spending more time at the library, if only for the ambience.

Noon soon arrives. Mom and I go into this little vacant kitchen behind the main checkout area. She thinks I've come to visit her, and why should I wreck her illusion? Besides, maybe this will get me back into her good books. She's been a bit of a snapping turtle with me lately.

Retrieving her sandwich bag and bottled water from the refrigerator, she sits down at the table and notices I've committed a slight sin. "Elbows off," she softly orders, and I instinctively obey.

Through the open door past her head the library bulletin board is clustered with colourful posters and illustrations, showcasing major community events. If only life could be as serene and fulfilling as all the libraries I've ever seen make it seem.

"So," I begin, with my hands folded on the tabletop, one leg jiggling with nervous energy, "have you hunted down all the criminals with overdue books?"

Mom laughs lightly at this dumb little remark of mine, then ceases and stares at me. "Odd," she comments. "You look so much like me, but really you take after your father." Her face has a deep kind of sadness that I can't quite read.

"I want to ask you something, Mom."

"Do you want half?" and she takes the first bite of her sandwich.

"No, thanks."

"Not hungry?" she mumbles back with her mouth full.

She always manages to throw superficial obstacles in the way of possibly more important things. Sometimes, it's very frustrating. The only strategy is to try again.

"Mom, I want to ask you something."

"Okay." She swallows from her bottled water. "Fire away."

"Let's say you were in a situation where everything seemed fine, but then you had these . . . suspicions, you know . . . that it wasn't like you thought. What if it was maybe awful, and you still didn't have the whole picture about what was really going on?"

Mom has put down her sandwich and is gazing into my eyes. "Suspicions?" she whispers.

"Yeah."

She's taking her time looking at three of the four dull red brick walls that are within her vision range for maybe a sign to bounce off them and into her head. Trouble is except for one wall, which has a solitary calendar, they're bare. She'd be better off glancing behind her through the doorway at the bulletin board. "Does this have anything to do with your father?"

"Huh?" All right, now I'm really confused.

"Look, Jim, I know I've been hard on you and Lisa these past couple of months, but I'm doing the best I can. Your father's going through some tough changes in his life, and he has to sort some things out on his own. I've known him since we were in high school. There's no doubt in my mind that he'll make the proper decision. Don't let your suspicions get in the way of your good judgment. Okay?"

Talk about coming out of left field. Slowly I say, "He'll make the proper decision about what?"

"Let's not go into it now. You and Lisa will know when the time is right."

Whatever decision she's talking about, I have an idea it's not quite as wacky as him telling us he's actually from the planet Gritzoid and that Lisa and I are half-aliens. All the same, I've got a bad feeling about this.

Now I'm farther away than ever from the other answers I seek. And I have a mountain of questions that need to be answered.

ROCK FIFTEEN

IT'S NOT LIKE IF I'D GET THE CALL, but when. She really lets it go for longer than I thought she would. Staying home I wait the rest of Saturday and all of Sunday morning, and even do some homework. Just before lunch the phone rings. Cynthia wants to get together at her place and talk over a few things. I tell her no, not in her house. She's very hesitant about where I want to meet her instead, but I don't budge. Damn it, I'm putting my foot down! Reluctantly she concedes.

WALKING THE FAMILIAR WAY, I realize I don't know much. Some people, even those my own age, have this world already figured out. They know how things work: the political business stuff, how to keep everything running smoothly, whom to bond with and all that—people such as Cynthia, for example. So why does she go out with me? I'm an idiot by comparison. Anyway, seems like they're born different, these people who possess this mysterious wherewithal. It's like they have built-in signals that we mere mortals can't see, except when they decide to flash them on and blind us to the point of near insanity.

One thing I know for sure is, at this moment, I'm standing in front of Lynda's Home Cooking in the brittle cold. A quick peek through the window shows me Lynda's bright face from behind her counter and the back of Renaldo's white head. Doesn't this guy ever leave? Not before Cynthia gets here will I venture in.

Over and over, thoughts with question marks are pounding through my brain. What the hell am I going to say to her? Should I turn on full blast my jet engines of accusations? Maybe I should ask her something simple first and slowly work up to the heart of the matter? Or will she immediately admit the truth and beg for forgiveness? Then again, I don't know the full story. I'm tense.

She parks her mom's BMW by the slushy curb of the street. Bouncing out she locks her door remotely, then looks my way. "Why wouldn't you let me pick you up in front of your house? You must be freezing." So casual, so everyday friendly, like there's nothing out of kilter.

I look into her steel blue eyes. My icy voice says it all, "I needed to cool down."

She frowns in amusement, as if I'm temporarily being silly or something, as if there's no importance in what I've just said. Brushing the front of my coat as she passes, she opens the door to Lynda's. "After you, let's get warm."

Now she's smiling, inviting me to imitate her. I don't. My expression is blank. I continue to study her for several seconds. Grimly I walk through the space between us.

I sit down at my usual table and Cynthia follows. This time I'm the one in charge and she'd better get used to it. There are a few other patrons scattered inside here. They're puffing away talking about the sad state of the world, unaware that they are worsening it with their poisonous cigarette clouds.

"Let me guess," Cynthia quietly speaks into my ear, "you secretly love second-hand smoke?" Oh, she's trying to be humorous with me. Won't work.

"Maybe." I'm a machine. No emotion is leaking out from me. When I start feeling stuff, that's when things get totally screwed up.

Again, Renaldo is yacking his head off to Lynda, " . . . and so I'm stuck at that bloody main intersection, and this goofball is blowing his horn! I tell ya, I could-a got out and busted his chops, then and there!" He's tough as nails for an old guy.

Lynda reminds me of those bartenders in black-and-white movies on TV. She's like an amateur psychologist for her patrons. "Relax. You're home at good old Fissure Rock, my dear."

"Yup," he grumps on, "till next weekend for the same fuckin' city shit!"

"Hey, hey," she whispers, scolding him, "be a good example. We've got a couple of school kids in here."

And Renaldo barks back, so we can hear also, "Well, why don't they go someplace else?" He doesn't even look at us to see who we are. Old curmudgeon would best describe him.

For the first time, Cynthia zeros in on the back of Renaldo's head. She can't hide her eyes opening wide in a split-second show of shock. They return to their normal size and her entire face is lost momentarily in sad thought.

We're here for a late lunch, and Lynda comes to us to get our order. "Is that Sally's daughter?"

My mouth opens first, "Yeah, it is." I'm solid as rock.

Cynthia continues to ignore my changed behaviour and is right back to her cheerful, professional self. "What's new, Lynda?"

At the sound of her voice, Renaldo cranks his head so he can identify the two school kids who have invaded his territory. He gives this deep groan like a watchdog recognizing something it does not want to confront. He turns away once more, slurps at his soup and grumbles to himself.

"You know what?" Lynda puts an arm over my shoulder. "This one would make a fine catch for a boyfriend. He's what I call an outsider regular. Real polite and handsome. Not an easy combo, these days." She laughs out loud. "Tell me, are you two an item?"

But Cynthia's attention lingers on Renaldo's presence in the diner. Finally she answers matter-of-factly, "Jim and I are in the same English class." Inwardly she seems to be fighting off her worry about where she is. Not wasting a further breath, she shows her teeth and orders, "May I have a tomato-and-lettuce sandwich on whole-wheat, please?"

"Sure, and how about young Romeo?"

"Coffee," I respond in the deepest voice I can manage. "Black." I've never had the crap without cream and sugar before. It doesn't matter since I don't plan on drinking it. Same English class! I'm suddenly reminded of Andy, of every cryptic thing he told me about this girl.

Lynda leaves us and Cynthia drops a barely audible bomb. "Jim, if you don't want to be around me anymore, no one's forcing you."

My jaw drops. "What?"

"The way you're acting. You insisted on me coming here when I told you I didn't want to. If you're more interested in Melissa or Karen, all you have to do is be honest with me."

Who are these girls she's talking about? I think I've heard their names when Mr. King calls out attendance. My head's been so completely full of Cynthia, from day one, there's nobody else who can fit in there. "You don't get it," I begin.

"No sense in excuses," she whispers. "You want to dump me? Do it now." Her business-like eyes bear into mine, nothing in them to show me any feelings whatsoever, but she looks in Renaldo's direction with incredible disdain. "I won't stay in this place any longer than necessary." She probably views 'this place' as a hangout for undesirables, those people who are beneath her. What a snob!

I can't hold back. "Cynthia, I'm pissed because you never told me about the FRATS website and Mr. Kween's perverted little message. Whoever he is, he can find out where I live. The name of my street and pictures of me are on there for the whole world to see! He's bought at least one video, so he knows what I look like."

My coffee and Cynthia's water are settled on our table, courtesy of Lynda, who returns hastily to her open kitchen to make the sandwich.

"Oh that," Cynthia waves her hand downwards. "Danny said you came over. I told him to get rid of the entry. He'll also delete your address from the roster, all right? Nobody will bother you. Danny really likes you, Jim. You're like a big brother to him." She sips the water in her usual graceful fashion. Nothing upsets her . . . except something about Renaldo.

"Are you telling me Dan put up that website by himself?" Even though I'm seething with anger inside, I don't come flat out and declare Dan an imbecile who's incapable of knowing a thing about computers—although this is what I believe.

"He and his friends managed to do it." Cynthia looks at me as if I'm the one out of sync in this scenario. Swaying her hand at the smoke drifting into her face, she turns to stare out the window.

Does she take me for a complete fool? She can't simply explain all this away! "You weren't at the library, yesterday."

"No."

I shake my head for an instant. "Where were you?"

She looks up at me like I've asked her something utterly unreasonable. "I was somewhere else. Jim, I do have my own life. Don't think you own me."

Lynda delivers the sandwich to Cynthia and walks back to say goodbye to Renaldo, who's getting ready to leave.

Once he's out the door, Cynthia's reaction is interesting. She sighs as if she'd been holding her breath the whole time he was in here. Now her only source of tension appears to be me—and the cigarette smokers who remain. Anyway she looks more clearly focused.

I go on with my offensive. "You never told me you were selling wrestling videos." My index finger unintentionally points at her.

She has to swallow some of her sandwich first. Finally she offers me a pair of confused knitted eyebrows. "Jim, you know we record the matches. You've never objected before." She takes another bite.

"The point is you didn't tell me you were selling them!" Once more my finger wags at her in the air like a wounded puppy dog's tail. "You and your brother are making money and I'm jobbing for free, is that it?"

Cynthia thoughtfully taps her fingers on the tabletop. "Is this what you're so worried about? You want a share of the profits? Do you really think Danny and I are making money for ourselves from the video sales?"

"Stop that!" There's a growl in my voice. "You're really good at changing the subject. You couldn't care less about what kinds of lunatics are buying your . . . products, and getting their little twisted thrills out of them."

Now Cynthia's ticked off at me. Her hands grip both sides of the table as she leans forward. "I thought I knew you better than this. You're not a lawyer, and I'm not on trial. But just so you know, proceeds from FRATS videos go towards the fundraising activities at school. Here you are, condemning me for contributing to charitable causes. What has gotten into you?"

Fumbling for words, that's what I'm doing right now. "I—uh, I didn't know that." I've screwed everything up. My face is turning red. Great job, Jim! See what a suspicious mind does for you? I wouldn't blame her if she broke up with me immediately.

Cynthia is so cool, though. "I'm sorry. I should have told you all this at the start." She reaches up and runs her gentle fingers through my blond hair.

My head turns to face the palm of her hand and my lips kiss it. "I'm sorry, too. I guess I was jumping to conclusions." Mom knows more than I thought she did when she spoke to me at the library, even if she was referring to Dad at the time.

"Now, I want to talk to you about something else," she says with light eagerness. Her hand retreats from my proximity. She's a beautiful unreachable fast-moving cloud.

"Uh, yeah?" I try to at least keep up with her shadow.

She stops for a moment. "Actually," she carefully begins again, "it's a request from Danny. He wants the main event to be you and him at Splinter Wonderland, the week before Christmas. I have 20 inquiries for this video already. If they all wind up buying it, we could raise $1,000, minus $100 shipping expenses, for a total of $900. Please say you will. Think about the library . . . and the swimming pool."

Her confident words lead me only one way. If I refuse her, I'm afraid I'll lose her. Skating on thin ice I say, "Sure." Really I'm too confused to say anything else.

"Yes!" Again her glittering white teeth are fully revealed. "You're the greatest!" I've heard her use that line before somewhere.

Lynda marches over to us, needing a break following her banter with the departed Renaldo. "Cynthia, I saw your mother passing by last week."

"Oh?" She's incredibly disinterested.

"Yeah, with a tall handsome man. Seen those two around a lot lately, walking along the street, here and there. He had on a bright yellow coat, real sharp looking. She seems mighty happy with him." Lynda bends over to talk in Cynthia's ear, loud enough so I can also hear, "It's been ten years since the divorce. Do you think this new guy might be the one?"

By now Cynthia has finished her sandwich and water and is reaching for her own coat. "I wouldn't know, Lynda," she answers as she prepares to depart. "Ready, Jim? I'll drive you home." She throws a twenty-dollar bill on the table. Talk about good tips!

Normally I would simply say okay and we'd be on our way. But I'm glued to my seat. You see, my dad's a tall handsome man, and he has a bright yellow coat.

ROCK SIXTEEN

I'M ALONE IN MY SISTER'S ROOM, seated at the computer, looking through the FRATS website. It turns out Cynthia is true to her words. Mr. Kween's message has been taken out, and my street name isn't part of the roster information anymore. Next I check to see if Andy's sent me any e-mail since he left. There are three messages from him, and an e-mail from someone else.

1) "Hey Jim: Well, got here safe and sound. E-mail me when you get a chance."
2) "Jim: Two weeks and no reply. Everything going fine? You can call me collect."
3) "Yo Jim: Chatted online with your sister and she said she'd tell you to e-mail me right away. Don't worry, I know I'm not the most interesting person. Have a great life. I understand. Bye."

Rapidly I reply to him: "Apologies! Lisa never told me you wrote and she hogs the computer almost 24 hours a day. Bad excuse, I could have checked it myself . . . only things have been kind of rotten up here. I'll get back to you with more soon, okay? Later."

Seconds after I click 'send,' I check out the remaining message. Opening it, I read: "Hi, sweet JimmyJobber. Guess you don't know how I got your e-mail address, do you? I GOT TO HAVE YOU. Let's hook up soon, awright? Your BIGGEST fan, Mr. Kween."

Before I know what I'm doing, I delete it immediately. The first time, on the message board, I was scared. This time anger is drumming inside me and I have to find a release! How can I fight what I can't see? Who is this guy? And now I realize that by deleting his message, I've just destroyed any evidence I had. Shit!

I switch off the internet connection and the computer itself.

Steaming determination thuds me down the stairs and walks me into the living room. Lisa is doing her pre-dinner TV viewing. She often sits with her ass on the floor, like she's doing now, wearing big old jeans and a large white sweatshirt. Her arms are crossed around her stomach and her fists clenched hard. My sister is deep into this rebel-without-a-cause get-up, and I'm fed up with it! On the upper part of her left arm is some weird, removable Satanic tattoo. She tells everyone who might believe her that it's permanent. Naturally Mom and Dad would never allow this. Instead she just re-inks it onto her skin everyday.

I'm a tree, planting myself firmly in front of the television. "I want to talk to you."

"That only makes one of us," she replies. "Get out of the way, Jimmy!"

Things have been bad enough for me at school today. I bombed another Science test, and in Gym class a great hulking moron smashed my shoulder into the boards while we were playing hockey on the outdoor ice rink behind the main building. And hey, it's only Monday. Finally with the unexpected e-mail from Mr. Kween, something inside me snaps. "Shut the hell up, you little freak!"

While Lisa's surprised eyes bulge out like a bug's, Mom enters via the kitchen. She doesn't say anything because this is all strangely new to her. My sister and I have never actually had it out before.

Lumbering to her feet, Lisa gnarls at me, "Who do you think you're talking to?"

"You're nothing but a pain in the ass to this whole family!" I scream, and this scene is getting a little too surreal. These words, are they coming from me?

Lisa snipes back with a sizzling bullet, "Oh, yes, you're one to talk, Jimmy! Why don't you tell Mom about how you wrestle with all the boys in town, so that old perv can see your pretty loser face on his computer screen?"

Oh God, I should have known. Never tangle with Lisa. She has true talent in confrontational moments while I can do nothing but wilt. I'm speechless.

Finally Mom thinks up some words to say, "One of you had better tell me what is going on." She's quite calm, considering the situation.

"Ask your boy wonder! I was just watching TV and he comes barging in—"

"Andy e-mailed Lisa and she never gave me the message," I explain.

Lisa argues, "Jimmy, you can check your own e-mail. He said he tried getting in touch with you before, but you never replied. What kind of friend are you?"

All right, she's got a point. I haven't been thinking too clearly recently. But I think that's understandable. I've had a lot on my plate. That's what Dad would say if he was here. He'd be on my side, but he's working late. Besides I just finished e-mailing Andy and hopefully patched up my neglect as far as he's concerned.

"I want to know," my mother begins, slowly pronouncing each syllable, "what all this talk is about wrestling and some old perv." She places her hands on her hips and studies me, then Lisa.

Seconds tick by slowly. Lisa suddenly tops my list of possible suspects regarding the true identity of Mr. Kween. Is she capable of such a sick prank? Beads of sweat pop out of my forehead. My sister looks into my eyes for the first time in a while, and I sense some of her anger lift.

Laughing, Lisa gently shoves me out of the way of the television. "It's nothing, Mom," she answers. "I just like messing with Jimmy's miniature brain."

Since she's now sitting on the sofa, shutting off Mom and me in the process, I continue, "Just a misunderstanding." What else is there to say?

I guess because I've kept my silence about Gerald and her, my sister has let me off the hook. So, even Lisa can't be behind all this. There truly must be a Mr. Kween out there.

Before she leaves us my mother walks over to me and whispers into my ear, "I don't like secrets in my own house, and I'm willing to bet that girl you go out with is somehow involved in this." In disbelief I look at her as she marches into her kitchen.

SPLINTER WONDERLAND awaits and I'm actually looking forward to it as I struggle into my winter clothes to face the crisp cold. Since neither Mom nor Lisa say goodbye to me, I leave without a trace of guilt. My family is not what it used to be. I don't need to rely on them for anything, especially not on my often-absent father. With Andy gone, I have no more heavy role to play, trying to stop him from committing suicide and all. I'm liberated! Basically I continue to hate wrestling, but in my boring life it's gradually become a kind of high (not to mention the occasional beer and pot that help bring out the buzz of the whole experience). And then there's Cynthia; enough said?

Outside, feathery flakes float down and cover me with their sparkle.

Walking along the street, I admit I'm on the paranoid side. Every vehicle yielding close to me sends a little alarm bell ringing through my brain. Hmm, is that Mr. Kween? Don't get the idea I'm some shaking bowl of jelly or something because it isn't true. With the strong workouts I put into Gym class five days a week, I feel tough enough all right. Also, wrestling for FRATS isn't exactly a cakewalk even if our stuff is half-rehearsed. Still I need to be better prepared to pound out this unpredictable maniac if he ever appears. Here's a smart idea: never let your guard down. This is definitely a longer trip than usual with the frost finding a way to bite through my glove protected fingertips.

CYNTHIA DOESN'T MIND as I brush off the accumulated white stuff all over her carpeted front hall. Like an old couple, we work together removing my coat, gloves, boots and putting them into the closet. After a warm peck on my thawing cheek, she informs me, "Everybody's all ready. Go on down." She adds, "I have to pick up a few things. Might be a while. Love ya!"

And she's gone, leaving me alone in this house where I only feel comfortable if she's in it. I move along to the basement door and steady myself to enter Wonderland.

ROCK SEVENTEEN

EACH STEP DOWN THE STAIRS brings me further confusion about this evening's plans. The whole roster has shown up tonight, and in my ears the guys are mighty pumped. There's a buzz of busyness in the air.

Someone says, "This is no mercy night! We're hardcore all the way! Screw those Shift Creek guys!"

Another one yells out, "Once we finish with 'em, they gonna know there 'aint no backyard fed in the world better than us!"

Finally I reach the bottom step that makes the lowest floor in the house visible. My eyes are tricked by a change of scenery. Yeah, the two bed mattresses are in place, this time with a blue tarp wrapped tightly on top like a tablecloth, and surrounding them are four vertical poles with three horizontal ropes attached to them. One cement wall is taken up by a huge sign that shouts: 'FRATS SPLINTER WONDERLAND . . . where only the brave WOOD dare enter!' For some reason two guys are taking this sign down.

"Jimbo, you're here." Joe, forever stating the obvious. He looks overly pleased, but not completely stoned . . . yet.

"Cool set-up," I hear myself say.

Dan's all business. "We did the first two matches. But the Shift Creek guys just phoned and challenged us to fight them on their own turf. We're goin' up there!"

Now I know what all the activity is about, with guys picking up stuff, packing in a rush. They're going to pop off for an unscheduled little field trip. I want to be here when Cynthia gets back. I don't buy into this wrestling obsession the way they do. In short I would prefer not to go up Shift Creek. "I'm staying," I notify them.

Dan's gelled hair, filled with spikes, seems to stand on end even more due to what I've just said. He glares at me like I'm his worst enemy. "Are you a little girl or what?"

It's Joe's turn. "Cynthia's gonna luv what we're plannin'. She's always sayin' to us we gotta do stuff that's spur-a-the-moment. You can ride with me, Jim."

I could insist on backing out but I don't, and it's not only because of what Joe said about Cynthia's approval. There's a morbid curiosity in me about Shift Creek, plus there never seems to be enough time for me to stop, think and make the right decision. I have to know what the place is all about. Besides it's only ten miles north of here.

RIDING IN FRONT WITH JOE inside his ancient SUV I have to tolerate the six guys cramped into the back, drinking beer, all encouraging him to go faster. He cooperates. This wouldn't be so scary if only the weather was better. Heavy falling snow and harsh howling winds hog the night. They make viewing past the headlights practically impossible. It's cold and dark. We're speeding, slip-sliding away on a barren highway. Everyone's laughing . . . except me. Exactly why did I agree to this, again?

About ten minutes pass. Joe turns to the right, and as near as I can figure his tires are now skating along a narrow road. On either side, in place of evergreens, I see trees covered in thick white pillowcases. Our bodies bobble up and down above the frozen stone surface that's covered with small crevices. We spin our way up an incline. Higher and higher into a tunnel of trees, where even the snow begins to look dark, I feel very alone and lost while my travelling partners eare rowdily appreciating this adventure.

Just before I can't take anymore, Joe brakes. A couple of guys pull out flashlights and I'm able to grab a glimpse of our location through the windshield. We're on top of a huge hill that seems to be where the world ends. About fifty feet below, a trailer park clutters up the space on one side and a frozen creek bed meanders along the other. Where we are with so many trees around us, their branches over us, I'm under the illusion that the snow has ceased its falling. Directly ahead is a big old dilapidated barn. The windows are boarded up, but a bright light sneaks out from under the slit of the only door. Atop the tin roof a small chimney is spewing black smoke.

As soon as the other cars catch up to us, everybody gets out to be greeted by the cold snapping air.

Dan races out of one of the vehicles towards the barn and shouts his taunts, like a smoke-breathing dragon in this unreal night. "Julian! Model-T! Bring it on, you losers!"

INSIDE THE HUGE STRUCTURE a wrestling ring rests in the middle of the floor. It is way more 'sophisticated' (if that word can be used in this place) than Dan's basement—or even backyard—pieces of construction. The overall shape of the barn's interior is similar to a toilet seat and somehow it's fitting. Raised up higher than ringside is the audience section.

There are about thirty guys milling around, all of them FRATS and Shift Creek wrestlers. I guess they'll be doing double-duty tonight: when not taking part in a match, they'll act as part of the audience. Makes sense. Who else, apart from me, would be insane enough to venture out in this weather if they weren't die-hard backyard wrestlers?

The barn is warm and it smells of beer, pot and piss. Everybody's rushing back and forth, in and out, setting up. Feeling off-guard I stand, watch and listen.

"Crank that music loud for the entrances!"

"Don't use no flimsy boards! We wanna split that mic with cracking sounds!"

This is a solid operation. A huge aluminium ladder leans against a corner of the barn, and there are about ten hockey sticks strewn about. I see at least one pair of handcuffs somewhere, but my attention is cut short.

Dan yells, "I'm gonna make the bladin' a s'prise for later."

Blading? What's that?

Joe's voice intended for Dan alone, "Whoa, guy, y'sure 'bout this?"

A Shift Creek voice responds, "What are ya, a wussy!" His tone is angry. I'm looking around a maze of moving males to identify the speaker. "He's my bro and if he wants to blade, he'll blade. Got a problem with that?"

I've spotted the guy who just said all this and he sure looks intimidating.

"No, Model-T," answers Joe meekly. "No problem." Joe wanders away.

Model-T is no taller than I am, but he's got a freaky frown for a face. If looks could kill, well, you get the idea. His brown hair is cropped really short and he has a rugged appearance that I wish I had myself. Not ugly, exactly, Model-T has . . . a commanding presence. I'm thinking no one would mess with me if I looked like him.

A new face enters carrying a cardboard box. "Let's get ready to rumble!"

(These clichés are killing me, boring me to death.)

The box contains several pairs of wrestling shorts. Some are white, the rest are black. A bunch of guys are already carefully searching for the right ones. "Hey, Julian," someone yells, "are you fighting tonight or just announcing?"

"Oh, I'll be ready for the Rumble at the end," he promises and drops the box on the floor. What remains of the throng sifts through this box like it's a shrine.

The Shift Creek wrestlers are changing into black shorts, while we FRATS members must put on the white ones. There are red name labels on the back of each pair. By the time I saunter over to the box, there it is: 'JimmyJobber.' As I follow the herd and remove my shirt and pants in favour of the white shorts that bear my wrestler nickname, I'm guessing Cynthia's hand is in here somewhere. Talk about prepared. This is no spontaneous challenge. Nice try, though.

After I change into the tight fitting shorts, Dan grabs me by the elbow. He says, "Hey, Model-T, this here's JimmyJobber."

Model-T looks me up and down, taking his time. "Cynthia goes out with this guy?" he scoffs then reconsiders. "Yeah, I guess a city prep boy is perfect for her."

I wonder if he's her ex-boyfriend, and I do my best to be polite, "Pleased to meet you, Model-T." I grin at his name.

His eyes burn holes into mine. "Call me sir!"

Why? He's only around my age. But I say nothing. I'm nervous.

Thankfully he calms down. "Dan says y'knew Andy Bradford b'fore he took off."

"Yeah." I'm bracing, ready to be further insulted, this time for my friendship with Andy.

Model-T waits. "Well?"

My eyebrows rise. "Well what?"

With solemn concern he asks, "How's he doin'?"

Dan breaks in, "Model-T, I wanna wrestle Jim first. Later we can do all the inter-fed stuff."

"Okay, little bro, you got it. This JimmyJobber won't give ya much trouble, that's for sure." Model-T chuckles and ruffles his hand through Dan's short spiked hair with real affection.

A bit annoyed Dan complains, "Aw, now I gotta fix the spikes again!" He rushes off to do that.

Julian takes his place at the commentator's table set up in one corner of the barn. He screams into the microphone: "Ladies and gentlemen!" (Odd, there are no ladies present.) "Welcome to FRATS' little Splinter Wonderland main event. After it's done, we can get on to what we're all here for, which is the Shift Creek Challenge. Anyway over there is JimmyJobber!"

This really crappy music starts playing, some childish tune I might've enjoyed when I was like eight years old. It nearly unnerves me and I'm not sure why, as I climb into the ring. The all-wrestler audience boos as I raise my hands over my head to show who I am. It's a part I play; I must play my part.

Out of the corner of my eye, I see Dan returning from his hair readjustment.

"And his opponent is . . . formerly FRATS' favourite brat,

Killer Dan, who now calls himself Rayvenous!" He steps into the squared circle. Instead of music, there's just the sound effect of a screaming raven and the crowd claps its hands approvingly.

Right away Dan runs towards me and delivers an elbow into my lower abdomen. I double over, winded and surprised. As soon as I see his foot coming toward my face for a kick, I grab it and twist forcefully, causing him to crash headfirst onto the hard canvas. This gives me time to catch my breath and think how I'm going to teach this little punk a lesson.

While he lies on his stomach, I straddle onto his back, grabbing his chin with my clenched hands and pulling back. I don't apply it too forcefully, but I know he can't get away. Making certain neither of the two cameras can record it, I quickly whisper into his ear, "What the hell are you doing?"

"This is wrestling for real!" he shouts back in anger. "Let's see what you're made of, soccer boy!" Dan's got a lot of nerve for somebody locked in a camel clutch.

Aware of the camcorder and its microphone, I whisper again. "Let's both chill. I don't want you or me to get hurt. Deal?"

"Awright," he whispers back and I release the clutch.

Things seem to be back to normal. I stand up and land a few fake stomps to his back. Dan sells them pretty good with painful-sounding groans.

Once he's standing, he reaches up and I'm in a side headlock. I'm hip-tossed onto my back and he hammers at my head with real punches. "Hey!" I protest.

He yells loudly so everyone in the barn can hear, "Don't step in the ring if ya can't take the sting!"

The audience roars with laughter. A chant of: "Ray-ven-ous! Ray-ven-ous!" repeats, and it sounds way past stupid.

Dan lets go and is on his feet again. "Get up, boy! Take your punishment!"

While I'm getting up with vengeance on my mind, he's gone behind me, and when I finally find him, he's holding one of those fold-up steel chairs and sends it colliding with my forehead.

Even though it's only the cushion part making contact, Dan uses plenty of force and I go down on my knees. I feel dizzy.

Julian rattles away at the commentators' table, but I can't hear a damn word he's saying and obviously I don't care. I have something more important to deal with here and now. Dan's bent on hurting me bad and the other wrestlers are happy to watch, even cheering him on. How do I get into these messes?

He grabs me by the hair, and I give him a good shot of his own elbow medicine to the abdomen. He rolls in pain on top of the canvas.

Behind me I hear a quick snap, followed by a sharp stab into my back. Swinging my head around, I see Model-T holding onto a broken hockey stick, grinning like a vampire. He looks on with pride at the damage he's just done, as I put my hand to my back and again sink to my knees. I'm bleeding. The seated wrestlers applaud and a few are using their deepest voices to repeat: "Blood! Blood! Blood! Blood!"

Dan takes advantage of Model-T's interference to elbow drop me on the back of my head, and I go down hard. There's no doubt in my mind; he's intent on maiming me. This kid's crazy, as in certifiable. I am facing real danger, and I don't belong here. Unfortunately I'm too hurt to move on my own. Dan forces me to my hands and knees. Before I know it, I sort of stagger onto my feet with him guiding me.

"Now I got him!" he screams out. The guys in the chairs clap. Dan scoops me up like he's going to body-slam me, but holds me in mid-air. "He's mine!" he reports to one of the camcorders. I try in vain to get away by kicking my legs in the air. Dan readjusts his hold and gets an even firmer grip in my crotch with the crook of his arm.

"AH!" I squeal. "You're squishing my nads!"

Lots of laughter erupts from the other wrestlers over that one. Next, Dan carries me over close to the ropes and urges Model-T to do a repeat with the broken hockey stick. "Open up that gash good and wide!"

Model-T uses the shards of wood at the end of the weapon

to dig away at my back even more. I'm yelping with incredible pain and anger, completely helpless. Several seconds tick on like hours before he drops me. On my way down he sticks his knee out, my back making hard contact; Joe's finisher has just been modified and outdone in terms of sheer torture. By the time my face is flat on the canvas mat, I notice fresh bloodstains on it—and the fact that I'm close to being unconscious.

I am eight years old again . . .

Laughter from above, a so-called friend straddled on my chest in his backyard. "*Hey,*" *he says is a strained and excited voice,* "*I bet I can do whatever I want to ya!*"

My eyes are faintly aware that Joe is walking slowly down ringside from the back of this large barn. He nods at me, wearing a serious expression that I can't understand. Everyone else out there in the crowd is smiling and laughing . . .

My so-called friend turns quickly around while on top of my chest and now his ass is just inches above my face. "*Better hope I don't fart, huh?*" *He laughs and grabs my knees, stopping my legs from flopping like two long fishes out of water.*

Before I know it, other boys and girls from our class are watching the action in his backyard. Somehow I'd blocked them out in other flashbacks; now here they are, all laughing at me as he reaches for the zipper of my jeans.

Dan has just been handed a little device, compliments of Model-T. While down on the mat, my head is grabbed and I am yanked like a rag doll into a sleeper-choke hold. My brain's getting fuzzier. I sense that what has just sliced through the skin above my eyebrow is a very sharp razor blade, the kind that's used for carpet cutting.

Whether I'm dead or dying, I don't care. I freak out! My hands go blind behind my shoulders and pull Dan's hair until he grunts and releases. Sitting on my butt, I swing around and land a hard right punch to his mouth.

He's stunned and backs away.

We both scramble to our feet.

My fists have minds of their own as they go to work on his face. He's down and bleeding. I keep at it. I want to kill him!

"Hey Ref? Do somethin'!" someone seated in the chairs section says.

The rest of them boo me. They stomp their feet and make these weird wild animal sounds.

That's when, from behind again, Model-T grabs another hockey stick. Running between the ropes and right into the ring this time, he breaks it over my back, pleasing the audience in the process, before disappearing in unnatural sadistic laughter.

I feel like a wounded deer as my bloodied-cut back makes contact with the cold mat. What have I done to deserve this? I lay there motionless, save for my heaving breathing, trying to wish everything away. My eyes close and I try to float out.

Eventually I sense someone standing above me. I wearily re-open my stinging sightseers and take in Dan's enraged face, the eyes of a madman—small spaces between his teeth oozing with blood. "Ya want it extreme? I'll give ya extreme!" He throws a folded-up steel chair on my stomach and gets ready to splash onto it.

Quickly I roll out from underneath it. He lands hard and begins cursing crazily.

The amount of blood dripping from my forehead is alarming. This can't be happening, I keep telling myself. My hand wipes away at the blood, but some of it trickles into my eyes anyway and I can barely see now. I know Dan will recover at any moment and I have to find a way to survive. That's the bottom line, here.

After I successfully struggle to a stand-up position, Dan knocks me down with a huge clothesline. On my mangled back, I can't move. He could easily pin me, but that's not what this is all about, is it?

That so-called friend, with everyone watching, and me worn out, all the fight gone from me, slowly pulls my pants down. "Let's see what ya got!" he giggles. Taking his time, he slides my underpants down and I am totally exposed for all to see. "Nothing much there!" he concludes as everyone joins in the laughter. Tears roll down my young face.

Model-T yells out with glee, "He can't do nothin'. Strip his shorts off!"

Camcorder One's getting closer. Close-up coming up.

Newly shocked, blind as a bat, still I'm not completely out of it. I can hear an argument that's suddenly been sparked. I recognize Joe's voice, and others shouting back at him. Exact words aren't clear. What's going on this time? What is time?

My shoulders are grabbed and I am dragged across the bloodied canvas to the edge. I'm taken (fireman's carry style) to a corner of the barn. I am trying to fight to get free. However I've lost strength and a lot of essential red fluid. Whatever's about to happen is going to happen.

I'M DUMPED LIKE A BAD HABIT onto a sofa in another room of the barn. I figure: Okay, since death is coming for me any second, I guess I have to first face this final and ultimate humiliation.

"Jim?" Joe's voice. He throws a towel at me and helps clean up my face, hands me my clothes. "Come on, get dressed. Fast! These guys are totally buzzed up. They're on something hard . . . it's really screwing with their heads. Hurry!"

"Oh God," is all I can sigh. He gets me a drink of water from somewhere. I feel like I'm going to puke, while I listen to the sharp words being flung out there in the middle of the barn.

Dan: "Who's got the handcuffs?"

Someone: "You didn't even use the ladder or boards yet!"

Making sure I'm dressed, Joe directs me by the elbow towards the door. We are able to edge towards freedom, undetected by the anarchy behind us. Joe puts on his coat and helps me with mine. "I'll drive you home."

Out in the night air again, no thoughts run through my head. Just cold.

I pass out before he starts his old SUV.

LUCKY ME, Mom and Dad aren't home by the time Joe helps me to sit on my bed. In fact since there's no TV set or music blaring loudly anywhere in the house and hardly any lights on, I figure my sister must also be out.

From nowhere Lisa appears in the doorway. Despite my weak condition, I notice her eyes are red and dry. How could she already be aware of what's happened to me? "Jimmy!"

Okay, I'm wrong. She's actually surprised.

"What—?" and she's lost for words. Imagine that.

"Hey there," Joe says to her. "Your bro here kind-a got into a fight tonight."

Lisa races to the washroom, hurrying back in with a soapy wet facecloth and gently applies it to my forehead. She's doing an excellent job as a dedicated nurse. I'm expecting her to do the old 'I-told-you-so' routine, about how I should have known about FRATS after she showed me the website message board and the whole nine yards. But she doesn't.

Joe speaks in his usual awkward way, "Um, I think maybe ya need to check out his back. Might need t'go to the hospital or somethin'."

Being very careful, they take my coat and shirt off.

I'm one-half pain and one-half passed out as Lisa yelps, "Jesus, Jimmy!" She says nothing more, realizing there's work to be done. After applying a bandage to my forehead, and getting another wet cloth to dab away the dried blood next to my spine, she reaches a conclusion. "I don't think you need stitches, but we better make sure it doesn't get infected." And she's off for the bottle of iodine.

With Lisa out of the room, Joe says, "Hey, bro, I better go. Looks like your sis' has everythin' under control, huh? She's great."

I look up at Joe, and think to myself . . . he's right. Yeah, she is great about all this. Maybe she'll grow up after all and be one of those people who can take control of things, such as emergency situations, anything that happens. Like Cynthia? There's a tarnished thought! Anyway I say a genuine thanks to Joe and he leaves.

The iodine stings really bad, but soon dissipates. Lisa carefully attaches a thick piece of gauze covering the entire cut. She hands me a cold glass of ginger ale, and after I take a sip or three I finally ask her, "Okay, Leese, you know how my night went. What's been going on here?"

Lisa becomes mute. This unnerves me. Again I notice her dry, red eyes. That's my biggest clue. She almost tells, changes her mind. "Jimmy, you better sleep now. You'll know everything in the morning."

She gets up, trying to leave my room with only that.

"No, Leese. No way." It's time I got some answers.

This time she stands at my doorway looking out into the hall, her back facing me. "Mom went to pick up Dad. He and Sally got really drunk again tonight."

I start to say, "Huh? I don't get—" Feeling dizzy again, I shut up.

"Sally was driving and a cop stopped them. They're both at the police station." She hasn't turned around to look at me.

Letting go a weak sigh, I say, "Dad better cool off on the drinking."

"Jimmy," Lisa says, impatience in her voice, "Dad and Sally have obviously been having an affair for a long time. Let's not pretend we still believe in Santa Claus. Mom left the house bawling her eyes out, and even I—"

She rushes to her own room, quietly shutting the door behind her.

ROCK EIGHTEEN

I THINK EVERYBODY, at some point, has been lost in a forest. Not a real one, just a place inside your head that screams: 'Too much!' I'm thinking Hansel and Gretel, as I see gigantic clumps of jellied moss jammed all over this sticky freaky forest. There are dangerous creatures lurking behind thick tree pillars. Birds and bugs make strange sounds to go along with strange smells only a forest can eke out. Back and forth from distant-distant land, I lay on my stomach, the pain from my back dulling away. Struggling between the real world and my dream ones, I can't decide which is worse.

At 1:35 a.m. the front door temporarily unlocks my unconsciousness. My parents (both very quiet) walk in and close up. Into their bedroom they go without a word. The tension between them wafts into my room through the small slit underneath my shut door. My former hero-father has sunken to the level of pond scum.

Now I've drifted back into that forest, where I'm inside some witch's dusty old house. She has warts all over her face, and on top of her counter she's got me roped and tied, ready to be boiled in a massive black pot of gluck.

"Ah!" she sings gleefully in a gravely voice, "I'm gonna taste me some JimmyJobber stew! Ha-ha-ha-ha!"

"Why?" I cry back, terrified. "Why?"

There's no answer.

I AWAKE TO SEE THE ALARM CLOCK reading 4:44 a.m. My back and forehead are aching. But my feet are fine. Walking my injured torso into the bathroom, I stand there in my underwear peering at myself in the mirror. The reflection is of someone who doesn't matter. I could be a fruit fly for all anyone honestly cares. The whole time I'm certain I've deserved this. A physical healing will take place, of course, returning my usual face to me, but I'll remain deformed inside. Stupid. Ignorant. Careless. Clueless. Absolutely useless. Hey, take your pick. And I can't stick around here. Got to make my move.

For reasons unknown, I feel I must get semi-clean. Using a fresh facecloth I wash the undamaged parts of my skin as best I can. I manage to shampoo, brush my hair. The image in the mirror already looks slightly better; appearances are deceiving. Splashing on cologne before going back to my room to begin the warm clothing process, I include two T-shirts for extra insulation.

In the kitchen, cereal and milk, toast and tea help revive me further. My mind is made up as I grab my backpack and sling it over an aching shoulder. I'm bruised everywhere, inside and out.

It's taken me a long time to do all this stuff. I don't get out the back door until 6:00 in a dark mid-December morning.

TOO NUMB TO FEEL the cold damp air, I trudge along. Not bitterly cold, I'm simply bitter, noticing nothing around me. A new vacancy occupies my mind. The world is a sickening and featureless place. This funk I've slipped into would really upset me if I thought I could feel anything except bad. But I believe it's impossible for me to feel any worse than I do right now; neither can I imagine an improvement coming along anytime soon, after all the crap that's happened.

LYNDA'S HOME COOKING normally opens at 6:30 a.m. Since I'm spotted out front, she lets me in a few minutes early and immediately starts with the questions. "Are you okay? What happened to your beautiful face?"

Shaking my head in place of replies, she catches on that I'm not too keen to talk about it.

I've soon got her famous mug of hot chocolate cupped between my hands as I sit at the barstool usually claimed by Renaldo. It's just Lynda and me this time.

I ask, "Can you tell me when the first bus leaves for the city?" The strained look on her face gets a little darker. "This is Sunday, luv. Bus doesn't roll in here until after noon."

Hearing this, I fade. Now what? Idiot I am, having never checked the bus schedule in this crazy town.

Lynda begins frying up eggs and bacon for me, the whole big breakfast deal. After I try to pay her she turns my money away with a wave of her hand. "Looks like you've paid enough somewhere else, last night. Eat up, get your strength back."

All I can murmur is a weak "Thank you." Amazingly I feel my spirits start to lift just so, and I begin to attack the full plate under my nose. Hungry instinct has taken mechanical control of me.

She leans in close, seriously concerned. "Whatever it is, Jim, remember you're young, you got a large future out there. Believe me, that's nothin' to sneeze at."

This startles me and I look up to see her face as if it's for the first time. I've always guessed Lynda's age at around forty. Now I'm thinking she must be sixty, maybe a bit older. Really it's hard to say. She could be almost old enough to fill in for my grandmother. My father's mom died young of a heart attack, and my dad's father died about a year after that—from the heartache of his loss is what my father says. So Dad was completely alone by the time he graduated high school, no brothers or sisters. Mom's parents were killed in a car crash before Lisa was born. I don't remember them at all. My mother's sister lives somewhere far away with her husband. I've never met them. Anyway figuring out people's ages (anyone older than my parents) is hard for me. I've got nothing to go by.

Renaldo stomps in. I can hear him stop dead as the door closes behind him. Maybe he thinks I'm going to turn around and fearfully surrender his seat to him. If that's the case he'd better do some more thinking. I'm in no mood for additional games.

I hear him grumble under his breath, "Bloody kids," and he sits a few bar stools to the right of me.

"Hey, big R!" shouts Lynda with exaggerated enthusiasm. "Got yours all ready for ya." She presents him with his steak and eggs, and God-knows-what-else is on that grease-filled plate.

I'm mildly surprised as the miserable old guy guffaws, "You're a lifesaver, Lyn. Did I ever tell ya that?"

"Only everyday, just about," she responds cheerfully.

I sip at my hot chocolate.

She gives Renaldo a steaming hot cup of coffee. "When you have to shove off?"

"Only got twenty minutes to get this down me. Runnin' late." He's pouring ketchup onto the one-hundred percent pure cholesterol that's piled up in front of him. He slurps a bit of coffee and farts.

Lynda waits until Renaldo has taken a few big mouthfuls and has lit up his first foul-smelling cigarette. Then she asks, "Mind takin' a passenger to the big city with ya?"

He looks up and exhales. "You closin' up for the day?" he asks hopefully.

This time she laughs, "Naw, the boy here needs a ride." She jabs at me with her thumb.

My eyes open wide. There's this incredibly long silence that shares space with the cirrus cloud of cigarette smoke hanging in the air. I do my best to protest, "Um, I—"

"Well okay," Renaldo cuts me off, and I'm in shock again, "but there's no stoppin' on the way. Got a deadline. Lose this crappy job and I'm on goddamn welfare."

Before I can break up their arrangement Lynda shouts out, "Oh, you're a real sweetheart down deep, Renaldo!"

He chuckles to himself, "Anythin' to keep ya happy, babe."

My fate has been sealed.

I KNOW NOTHING ABOUT CARS, never mind trucks. The huge beast of a vehicle Renaldo drives is plain intimidating. After climbing aboard with my backpack and closing the passenger door, I'm struck by his ability to shift from gear to gear and steer his monster through the narrow streets of Fissure Rock towards the highway. He could probably do it blind-folded. There's a flurry of further gear shifting as the big machine nudges onto the vast asphalt stretch leading back to where I came several months ago. My great escape begins.

All is quiet for a long while. The eyes of my driver seem crazy-glued to the highway directly ahead. He doesn't smoke inside the cabin, and I feel slightly blessed for small mercies. However I'm beginning to feel cold and uncertain. Looking at the stripped trees outside and the hard black surface we're riding upon, the throbbing pain throughout my body regains my attention. I can't let this nagging second-guessing get to me, though. My city mission, which will remain undisclosed for now, consists of three things.

I decide to break the ice between us. "Is your name really Renaldo?" Soon as I say this, I realize that I've never spoken to him before.

He delays, not turning the position of his head one-inch. "No. Renny."

"Oh." I conclude he's not too talkative when driving.

A short pause and then, "What about you?" he interrogates. "You got a name?"

After I answer, he nods. Silent seconds slither along.

"Jimmy, eh?" The truck's powerful old engine rattles the cab's interior loudly.

"No," I correct him, "Jim."

He smiles in an odd way. "Call me Renaldo . . . or Renny. Whatever."

But I don't intend on calling him anything. I am the one who doesn't want to chat now. There's something about his tone, something wrong. Maybe I'm psychic, maybe paranoid. The other cars on the highway provide me with some distraction. That's what I need plenty more of at the moment, good old reliable distractions. I try various things (memorizing numbers and letters on license plates, counting same-coloured cars, and so forth). The trouble is there aren't enough vehicles on the highway this early in the morning to hold my attention.

"So tell me, Jimmy," he starts up again with new boldness, "who you runnin' away from? Hope ya didn't get that Cynthia girl knocked up." His disgusting laugh-delivered words are followed by deep stomach-churning coughing.

Inside my mind I'm half-hoping he chokes to death. Mentally I begin adding up all the white birch trees that appear on the roadside among the pines, next to the ice-covered granite rock, and I ignore him altogether.

"Jesus H. Christ," he moans, "y'aint deaf. I asked you a question, boy!"

Emphatically I state, "Do you think you could possibly mind your own business?"

Renaldo flips out with a humorous roar, "Whoa-ho, if that 'aint the coffee pot callin' the tea kettle black!"

"What's that supposed to mean?" I am curious in a cautious way. I've lost track of my interest in the birches. They're hard to pick out when surrounded by thick blankets of snow, anyway, the sons of birches.

"You come and take over my stompin' grounds and y'expect me to be mindin' my own biz? You sure are somethin' else! As for that Cynthia gal, she can do better than the likes of you and that's for sure!"

He's got the truck in high gear now as I try to slow down this conversation. "Sir, I'm really not looking for an argument. It's just . . . I've got a load of stuff on my mind, right now, you know?"

Renaldo glances at me quickly, gives an evil smile, then lowers his voice. "Yup." With that, I'm thinking he knows way more than I want him to, but I can't explain it.

Thankfully a prolonged silence has begun. I savour it.

STRONG WINDS SLAP SNOW off tops of rock walls on each side of the highway. We've been on the road for close to an hour.

My view is that both of us are on edge. I like it during the lengthy time we stop talking. And of course all good things must come to an end.

"Hey," he finally asks casually, "got any ideas what you want outta life?" (Renaldo, the school guidance counselor? Somehow I can't picture it.)

"Peace and quiet," I say, smugly satisfied with my stoic reply.

"C'mon, for real," he snorts. "You can tell Uncle Renny."

"Don't know." Before I'm able to stop myself I unleash with the truth, "Maybe a writer."

Because some wet snow has begun to pile up in front of our eyes, he switches on the windshield wipers. "Writer? Hmm." His hatchet-worn face is wrinkling up more than usual as he considers my answer. "Course ya know, them writers, they're . . . different. Screwballs. Are you a screwball, Jimmy?" I practically pray for the truck's rattling engine and windshield wipers to be the only sounds I hear for a while; however, he goes on being creepy. "Yeah, I bet you're different from them other bozo boys in town. I'm wonderin' how different."

I don't like where he's headed, even though I don't know where exactly that is. This isn't a normal talk you would have with a guy who's roughly sixty years old. "I'm not different," I make myself sound clear. "I like writing because it's fun." Hopefully that'll shut him up.

The rocks disappeared some time ago. Open flat fields covered with snow and skeletal trees have replaced them as cold unsightly scenery. A few more cars pass us. Another silence has arrived. It doesn't give me much relief, quickly travelling on.

"Fun?" Renaldo suddenly blurts out. "Yeah, sure, you're young. Everything's fun! Ya know what? In no time you're gonna be old." Using one hand that's momentarily free of the steering wheel he snaps two of his fingers, "Like that!"

I look out the side window for something to concentrate on. He's going somewhere bad with this; I can feel it. I don't plan to participate.

A knowing chuckle comes from deep in the pit of his gut once again. "Nope, you don't like that, do ya? Can you believe I was ever your age? And it don't seem like so long ago neither." He waits for me to say something; he can forget it. "Am I scarin' ya, Jimmy boy?"

I turn to look at him and the shark-like slits of his eyes connect directly with my line of vision. For a split-second my insides are jarred. Still I keep on my blank bored mask. Watching straight out the windshield, where snow rushes down in a big white flash, I sink lower in my seat. There's always a way out of a tricky situation, especially before it goes too far. Isn't there? I think, and I think, and I think.

"Cat caught yer tongue, there, boy?" He laughs, coughs, and then lights up a cigarette in the middle of driving. A few puffs, and he mumbles with intense dislike, "Goddamn punk."

Staring ahead at the highway unfolding in front of me, I am hypnotized by the wipers moving the heavy-falling snow left and right. The old guy's playing a childish game, like a schoolyard bully. Taunting me, he's thoroughly enjoying himself. Somehow a really good question pops into my head. I decide to go for it. "If you hate me so much, why are you driving me to the city?"

Renaldo sighs and though I don't see him, I figure he's doing some heavy thinking. He whispers darkly, "Who says I'm gonna?"

My ears perk up, scolding hot. Inhaling a big silent breath of polluted air, I swallow hard. Talk about crazy, I venture into this shady area he is wallowing in. "What do you want from me?" Inside I'm petrified. While I turn to take in his ugly profile, he peers out through the front windshield that's being bombarded with snow.

"Way I see it," he says in a playful manner, "me and you gotta have a talk. Man to boy." He knows he's in the driver's seat, and he smiles at me like someone insane.

"A talk?" I repeat, scratching my forehead for something to do. Anything at all will do, as long as I don't let him see how totally frightened I really am.

"Yeah," he goes on in his gruff teasing voice. "For starters, anyhow. And I can teach you a thing or two about real life. That's what kids yer age need, some toughening up! Ya gotta learn it's a cold hard world out there."

My heart hiccups a beat.

"If you don't cause me no trouble, I might jus' drive ya to the city after that. Nothin's free in life, y'know!"

I try to sound bold and in control, "Maybe I'll get off right here and hitch a ride with someone else."

Renaldo shows me the big wide grin spread across his spooky face and says, "Ya think you're gonna jump out at the speed I'm goin' and stay alive?" He pauses. "Go ahead, Jimmy-boy! Let's see how you make out. Best you can hope for is broken bones. If the fall don't kill ya, the cold will for sure!"

Analyzing my next move, I wonder: Do I even have one? Do I dare say anything else? Finally I ask, "What is this?"

Adding to my dread he responds, "This is the only place you're safe right now! Imagine that, eh?" He swiftly changes topics. "Hey, what kind-a sports does little wannabe-writer Jimmy like to play?"

This is all way too weird. There's not a thing I can do, of course. Just sit here and listen to his drivel. As far as I'm concerned, Renaldo's questions are rhetorical.

"I got it!" he speaks out in a fake-friendly voice. "I bet you're a lightweight boxer. How else could'ja get all them bruises and that cut on your forehead, huh? Geez, you must-a got beat bad."

Without looking in his direction I feed him an ancient catchphrase, "You should see the other guy." Sensing his head turning to glance my way again, I add a smile for maximum effect.

More derisive laughter comes out of him, "Whoa-ho! Here I'm thinkin' I got me a real nice passive boy. Tough guy, eh? A challenge don't bother me none. 'Course, could be you're all talk."

Nervous as hell, I clasp my hands behind my head and stretch out, pretending to be as comfortable as a cat next to a cozy fire. When you're all out of bravery, bravado will have to suffice.

"You're the one doing ninety-percent of the talking, Renaldo." I'm taking a hell of a gamble because my options are few, running on empty.

While Renaldo gives the old "He-he-he," I've already got him figured out.

ROCK NINETEEN

RENALDO BREAKS HIS OWN RULE. We're halfway to the city when he tells me he's "got to have coffee an' a crap." He gears down with brutish effortlessness, bringing the dinosaur-age truck to a halt at one of those highway truck stops.

I'm ready to bolt and try to get some help. With a quickness and strength that startles me once again, Renaldo grabs my left wrist and throws a definite warning into my ear. "Now you listen good! Everybody in there knows me. It don't matter what you say to them, they 'aint gonna believe ya. They'll think you're nuts! All you got to remember is you're my nephew."

No longer able to hide the terror shaking in my voice or on my face I whine, "Why are you doing this to me?" The hold he has on my wrist is hurting me bad. "Please let go," I beg. I'm almost in tears.

To further amaze me, he releases his hold immediately upon my request. Renaldo's rock solid glare erupts into utter joy. "Ha-ha-ha! I really had you goin' there, didn't I, Jimmy?" Seeing my bewildered face he laughs again. "Yup, you took the bait, all right! I was only foolin' you the whole time, boy!" He even pats my shoulder. "Come on, let's grab somethin' to eat. Order what-cha want, on me." Practically bouncing out of the truck, he walks toward the restaurant without giving me a second look. Is this true? Renaldo expects me to believe that everything he said to me was nothing other than a sick, twisted joke?

I do follow him inside the restaurant and we occupy one of the orange booths. My head swims as I sit opposite him, trying not to look at his smiling face. There are other people inside the place and I notice no one says hello to him. Am I safe, after all? Looking out the large window I can see we're in the middle of nowhere, unless you might want to call 'somewhere' an endless stretch of snow-covered road with white fields and trees to match on either side. A radio is playing loudly and some obnoxious deejay notifies everyone about a great big blizzard on its way. Yay, my sister might say.

Having to put up with the radio is one thing, but there's also a giant TV screen in the corner pounding away. Guess what's on? Domination Wrestling (DW—another "professional wrestling" venue, a competitor of UDW). I stare at the screen as one of the big guys power-bombs his comparable opponent onto a board between two chairs. There is a stomach-turning, cracking sound as he goes through the piece of lumber. No doubt this was one of many more things planned for me last night by Dan and his gang, had Joe not rescued me. Then the TV program prepares to replay the move in slow motion.

My frown makes Renaldo turn his head to identify the cause of my latest dislike. "What's-a matter, don't Jimmy like wrestlin'? I thought you would've loved wrestlin'. Ha-ha!" The way he says this or the way he's looking at me, whatever, it's like he's just given himself away. Before all I had to go on were suspicions. Now as I add up everything, it seems I have some very strong evidence.

Alarm bells ring inside my head. I try not to quiver, trying hard to stay intact.

"Ya know," he starts drinking the full coffee cup after dropping in three sugar cubes, "I'd give just about anythin' to be your age again. Do some-a that-there wrestlin'. Time of yer life!" He continues to pelt me with this changed over-friendly performance. "How old are ya, anyhow?"

Naturally I don't respond right away. Wasn't it only a few minutes ago he had me all but convinced everything was a big joke? Following this coffee-and-crap stop, I would have gone back into the truck with him and . . . no, I don't want to think about it.

"Thirty," I finally fire back, and I take an arrogant gulp from the free glass of water I ordered. Truthfully I've frightened myself with this flippant reply of mine.

Although he's stopped smiling, he retains a strangely amused tone. "Smart ass," he whispers roughly. Renaldo leans back and lights another filthy cigarette. "That's what you is. Nothin' but a little smart ass." He exhales carcinogens into my face.

Having reached the end of my fuse, I decide to blow his cover. "Yeah," I sigh in the heaviest way I can possibly whisper in return, "and you sure must have a lot of time on your hands, man! Don't you, Mr. Kween?" I'm glaring ferociously at him, to hell with my fear!

If only certain expressions could be exchanged for dollar bills I'd be instantly rich. Renaldo's face is frozen. I've successfully screwed up whatever sneaky plans he had for me. He's like a fish out of water, flopping around helplessly. No one can wiggle out of this one, especially not a dumb-ass like him. But I must give him marks for effort. "What the hell did'ja call me?" There's supposed anger in his voice and eyes, and do I detect a tinge of guilt? Hmm, seems I've hit a nerve.

"You heard me," I answer back with authority. "I know who you are. Surfing teenage backyard wrestling websites, writing disgusting things on the message boards and e-mailing me! You're a real sick-o!"

The big fat cat is out of the bag and no way can he deal with it. Renaldo's shoulders rise and he's got on a big-time scowl that seems to swallow the rest of his face. I figure he's going to slug me. Big deal. His hoarse throat finds sour words, "You gone bonkers, kid." He's silent for almost a full minute. Then he says, "I gotta go check the plumbing."

As I watch him enter the washroom, I'm up on my feet and over to another booth where a man and his wife are getting ready to leave. "Excuse me," I ask, "are you heading for the city?"

"Sorry, son," the man answers, "we're going north."

I search around and discover that everyone else is busy eating. That means no immediate alternative ride. There must be a place to hide.

OUT INTO THE WIND-BLOWN SNOW I go with my backpack, scrambling to the rear of the restaurant where there are no windows.

Already my footprints are being covered up by winter's white stuff (God bless Mother Nature, again!). Renaldo won't think to look for me here. It's freezing like I've never felt before. The cold cuts clear inside my hurting bones. I ask myself that same question from earlier this morning: What have I done to deserve this? It really is happening, so I must have done something wrong.

Peeking out at the highway, I see the same man and woman I spoke to moments ago now inside their car driving north. Cursing myself, I know I should have gone with them in the same direction. I could have returned home and told Mom and Dad, and . . . I recall the nightmares of the night before, both real and imagined. Time to grow up. Going home isn't an option, it's history. I'm on a mission.

Next I hear Renaldo's unmistakable voice shouting from near the entrance: "Hey, kid! Jimmy! Jim! Where the hell are ya?"

Another man's voice, a whisper in the whistling snowy wind, suggests something to him. "Sir, like I said, your nephew probably grabbed a ride with the couple that just left. I saw him talking to them—"

Renaldo cuts in harshly, "Long's he's not freezin' his nuts off somewheres, what do I care?"

The other man's a bit miffed, "You're welcome, buddy!" He jumps into his little car and putters away, leaving Renaldo alone out front.

Shivering all over I yearn for the sound I want to hear. When you're waiting for something so crucial, it always takes so damn forever.

My brain's pendulum sways, Tick . . . tock . . . tick . . . tock.

An explosion sounds.

I jump, a cat electrocuted.

No, hold on, it's the sound of salvation.

Yes!

The truck's engine has started. That rusty metallic monster soon snakes along the highway in a southerly direction. From the far distance, my eyes pinpoint Renaldo's head looking left and right, trying to find me on the roadside. I won't go back into the restaurant until I'm certain his vehicle is well past the horizon. Meanwhile I've become an ice sculpture.

BACK INSIDE THE RESTAURANT I'm warm and boiling. That is, I feel like such a coward! Running away from the bogey man! Little, useless, scared Jimmy! Why didn't I kick his ass? My inner man has suffered horrible damage. After all, Renaldo is an old geezer, tough as nails or not! I bet if Cynthia's little brother were in my shoes, he would've grabbed a steak knife or something and carved him up like an obese turkey for FRATS Bloody Thanksgiving event in the fall. Dan takes crap from no one, got to hand him that.

Knowing me I could keep punching myself like this for hours, but a woman about Mom's age approaches me.

"Hello," she begins.

"Yes," I answer. "I mean, hello." My mind's all fogged-up.

"Did I overhear you ask someone for a ride into the city?"

I nod like an obedient pup.

"Well, I'm leaving now. If you want—"

"Thanks!" I interrupt her. This, I figure, is a chance with much less risk involved. "Very nice of you."

We walk out together, and in no time I'm on the road again.

THE OPPOSITE OF RENALDO, this lady does not talk about anything more important than the weather. I'm in love with this drive, as the blizzard conditions slowly dwindle down to light snowfall. I never do find out her name, nor does she mine.

IT'S LIKE SPRINGTIME HAS SPRUNG EARLY when I see the familiar buildings of the city approaching. A refreshing change from the barren landscape surrounding Fissure Rock, which offers only fragmented features of civilization. The clinical certainty of the thirty-floor cement hospital complex on the urban outskirts, next to a park and ravine, is a healthy sight for my eyes. Nearby houses, in slightly different styles, huddle within an easy walk to small plazas. Everything's compacted. The office buildings, the traffic and throngs of people serve as chicken soup for my suffering soul. It's almost as though I've floated up to heaven. In more detail, my mind begins to plan out the three things I must do.

ROCK TWENTY

THE FIRST THING I'm determined to get back on track is Sideline. Just like Dad lied over and over about working late, it was probably his idea to give away our family pet. As I remember it he never was too gung-ho about cats. It's really bad news when the guy you've admired all your life lets you down. For all I care, Dad can screw off with Sally if he wants to, but why should Mom, Lisa and I be deprived more than necessary because of his affair? I'm raging inside!

Anyway this woman driver lets me off right in front of the Ganderwort's house. I get out, and she wishes me well. I thank her at least three times. On home turf... even the pollution smells great! Also, the snow has stopped falling. Having lugged my backpack up the driveway, I knock on the door.

Mrs. Ganderwort opens it. She doesn't seem very surprised to see me. Maybe older people train themselves to expect surprises.

"Is that Jim?" (I've always wondered why people state the most obvious things, because she knows it's me.) "Come right in, dear," she says, like Hansel and Gretel's witch in my bad dreams.

"Hi, Mrs. G. How have you been?"

Acknowledging my entrance, Mr. Ganderwort shuffles into the living room as if he's balancing himself on a sheet of slippery ice. He's wearing worn green slippers that make a strange swishing sound on the smooth carpet. Standing there in pajamas and bathrobe, he says nothing. While his wife hasn't changed at all in only a few months, his face is way older than I recall it.

I don't mean to be rude, but my eyes are busily scanning the floor.

Mrs. Ganderwort catches on quick. "Oh, I think I know

who you've come to visit." She smiles like she's talking to a seven-year-old. I take off my boots in the front hallway. Then, almost launching me out of my socks, she screams out loud, "Snowbell! There's somebody here to see you, Snowbell!"

To my amazement Sideline comes to her. He circles about her ankles, not paying me the slightest attention. And where does she come off changing his name? She's brainwashed my old pal to the point where he doesn't remember me. I'm nothing, just another human being invading his territory.

I don't know what to do or say next as I stare at my former cat who sits purring beside her feet.

Finally to break the silence, my hand reaches out and I take a few steps towards him. Sideline (Snowbell, whatever) runs away and out of the room.

"Well," says Mrs. Ganderwort nervously, "cats are funny that way, I suppose."

Old Mr. Ganderwort has some stumbling words for me. "I think I know you, don't I?" One look into his eyes, and I can tell no one's home. Talk about sad. And so fast.

Admittedly, the first part of my mission is a major failure. Sideline is no more.

"You look . . . tired, Jim. Please sit down," the kind old woman says. "We want you to stay for tea." There's a twinkle of my nightmare witch's manipulative eyes in hers.

I'm a wee bit spooked, especially after what I went through with Renaldo this morning. "Oh," I say, "no thanks, Mrs. G. I have to go a few places. I'm just visiting for the day. Nice to see you both again, though."

She goes with me to the front door. "You will come back later today, won't you? We certainly do miss our former neighbours."

"Sure," I say, "of course." Anything to get away.

"And naturally, you'll want to see the cat one more time?" She's really pressing this coming-back thing, although she hides it with a sly smile. "Goodness, where is it you're going in such a rush?" The dismay on her face equals what's inside my mind.

Putting my boots on, I'm ignoring her prying for more information. No way would she understand where I'm about to go, plus it's none of her business. More definitely I state, "I'll be back."

"Before it gets too dark?" she adds. The number of worry wrinkles multiply on her face.

"Promise," I affirm. When I tell her I'll leave my backpack behind, she's relieved.

From the living room Mr. Ganderwort's feeble voice calls out, "Did you bring me any mail, sir?"

EXITING HER DOORWAY, and stepping down the front stairs, I'm off to tackle part two of my three-fold mission here in the city. I've almost shaken off the whole Renaldo experience, as it recedes in my mind.

Bryan, Mason, Wendy. I've tried to drop all three from my memory bank ever since I had to suddenly tear apart from them to move up to Fissure Rock with my parents. There's no sense starting out fresh in a new place if you're still moaning inside over leaving your friends behind. This time things are different. I'm thinking only about them as I walk several streets south. It's well into the afternoon now, and warmer. Although I'm not so sore, little darts of pain regularly remind me I'm far from fully healed.

Bryan used to make me laugh all the time. A crappy swimmer, he would make out like he was way worse than he really was, splashing away uselessly in the pool, exaggerating his imperfect skills like a wet clown. I'd point at him and chuckle, suggesting he try out for a comedy show on TV or something. Pretending to be angered by my remarks, Bryan warned me not to make fun of him, or else! This made me laugh even harder, and I'd forget for a while that I didn't get picked for the swimming squad.

Mason and Wendy were practically married. She was quiet around me, with a Mona Lisa dark face that looked like she was constantly philosophizing about the meaning of life. At the same time, Mason and I would kick the soccer ball back and forth. We were both on the school team; he played goal. We'd be in the park, and I'd be taking practice shots on him. During these one-on-ones, even though Mason was fantastic in net, I'd still manage to kick a few goals in by law of averages. Each time I did, I'd let rip with a huge holler, jump up and down, my fists raised triumphantly to the sky. Really rubbing it in, I was just joking around. He'd always end our get-togethers with funny one-liners; for example, "Come on, Wendy! Since Jim's such a hot dog, let's leave him alone so he can relish himself!" They'd walk off together, Mason in a big imaginary huff.

Remembering I grin, as a franchise of the Hamlet's Hamburgers chain nears. Suddenly I'm hungry.

THE PLACE IS THRIVING as usual on this late Sunday afternoon, creating difficulty for me to hear myself think. That's fine. I figure I do enough thinking to make it a bad habit; I deserve a break today. Besides I'm looking for my friends.

Bryan is first recognized. I spot his wiry black hair and large skinny nose that goes with the rest of his thin body. With him are two other guys I've never seen before. They both look very ordinary, with their bomber jackets on. Last time I saw him Bryan was a loner except for Mason, Wendy and me. For company he relied mainly on me.

I footslog to where he's sitting at the other end of the restaurant. He soon sees me and his eyes enlarge, "What happened to your face?"

Showing him my teeth are still intact, I shout out above the music and other voices, "Glad to see you, too, bro!" Then I slap the shoulder of his ski jacket.

It's strange, Bryan reels back, not enough for anyone else but me to notice. He introduces his two buddies and we do the old fist-tapping handshake thing, saying to each other, "Hey." Their faces remain serious.

The bright blue and yellow interior—and the unmistakable

delicious aromas of dead burning animals—inside Hamlet's Hamburgers comfort my reawakening senses. This is our old hangout. I ask Bryan where Mason is. He answers that he's probably at home.

"I think I'll call him, and see if he and Wendy will come over."

Before I head for the telephones Bryan responds, "Oh yeah, he'll like that a lot." His two friends snicker about something they find funny.

Although there's no mistaking the sarcasm in his voice, I don't stop. Deciding a reunion is exactly what the four of us need, I am being proactive again, back in my own element.

As it turns out, speaking to him on the phone, Mason is unwilling to make the short trip (Hamlet's is maybe a five minute walk from his house). He uses a few flimsy excuses that I easily shoot down and finally I get him to agree to join us. These are the good old days again, with me as their leader, the way it should be.

I buy myself the Ophelia Burger with cheese, onion rings and a hot chocolate.

EINSTEIN WAS RIGHT ABOUT TIME. An hour can go by quickly or slowly, but the one that stretches out before Mason and Wendy finally get here lasts one minute past forever. It drags on mostly because of Bryan and his two pals, whose names I can't recall. This has got to be the longest day of my life, as I gobble down the last of the meal on my tray. I go back for a cola, then return to face my old friend and his new ones.

Beginning with a pinprick Bryan asks me, "So how's life in that three-cow town of yours?" He sneers, showing his big pink gums.

"Great," I pop back, "we save a load of money milking cows instead of using store-bought."

Then Pal Number One pipes up, "Yeah, but dude, don't-cha find it kind-a hard tellin' the difference between a cow and a girl?" He chortles like a blithering fool.

"Naw," I dismiss him coolly, "do you?"

"Bry's told us plenty about Jim Bridgeman," Pal Number Two informs me, almost threateningly. He has a square jaw and a compact build.

Following last night and my Renaldo experience earlier today, any shots fired by these two nobodies aren't going to upset my apple cart. "I must be very interesting." My smile prevails.

Pal Number Two keeps at me while I watch Bryan slip away for another cola. "He doesn't exactly make you sound like a friend." He takes a few steps closer to where I'm standing.

I shrug and sip on the straw. "Maybe there's something wrong with your hearing," I suggest with a sudden burp. I decide, try as he might, there's nothing he can do that'll scare me.

The music's loud, people are talking all at once, burgers are sizzling away on the grill, and I'm doing my best to deflect the hostility being targeted at me by these two head cases. Hamlet's has always been a happy place, and I won't allow anyone to ruin my fine memories.

Pressing his point, Number Two literally bumps against me. We're about nose to nose as he talks on, "Hey, cement-head! Maybe what's wrong is your attitude."

I sit down, making sure not to cross my arms or legs. Body language can be very important in these confrontational situations. "Okay," I hang onto a relaxed tone. "Please, tell me, what mistakes must I correct in my attitude?" I feign amusement, feeling in control.

"Like what you're doin' right now!" bellows Number One, all red-faced. "Actin' like your King of Ever'thin' and all!" (His pal's grammar is way better.)

"Well," I give another shrug, "we are at Hamlet's. Somebody's got to be king."

To his credit, Number Two focuses on the issue at hand. "You sure like to be the man, don't you? Is that why you came back, to brag to Bryan about how great you're doing up there in your hick town? How many goals you got? How many trophies?"

I think to myself, if this guy only knew the truth behind my Fissure Rock fiasco. But he's caught my attention for another reason. What he's saying right now, is this the way Bryan really sees me, maybe the way he's always seen me? When I lived here, did I give off the impression to my friends that I was a self-adoring hot dog? If so, it was never on purpose, I swear. Still I can't lose face. "Sure," I boldly answer, "what other reason should there be?"

"Since you left he's got better quality friends."

Not letting it show, I'm struck by this statement. Number Two's words have smacked my head as surely as any chair swung by Dan the night before.

Mason's voice suddenly attacks from behind, "Something's rotten in the state of Denmark."

Here at Hamlet's Hamburgers, we used to do these puns on Shakespeare all the time, so what Mason's just said doesn't surprise me. I veer around to look at him, preparing to give him a welcoming smile. His expression blocks my will. Actually, both he and Wendy look down at me like I'm bad news.

Wendy herself says, "So how long are you staying?" Her disinterested tone and her eyes infer that she hopes my visit's a brief one.

"Hey Jim," Mason seals the envelope, "you buying for a change?"

Now it occurs to me that in the past each one of my old friends has taken turns paying for everyone's meals, or beverages at least, but not me. Was I a cheapskate? It wasn't on purpose. Thinking back I know it was just a matter of slipping my mind, or else I was short on money at the time, just like I'm short on words at this moment. I'm not a bad guy, really.

Bryan returns with his drink refilled. "Hey, guys." His smile isn't directed anywhere near me.

As Mason and Wendy, and Bryan and his two new friends talk amongst themselves, I get feeling really panicky. Have I been transported back into some 1950s black-and-white horror flick? Feels like it. Everyone has turned into zombies, except for me, or is it the other way around? If I felt out of place in Fissure Rock, I've just been more rejected here by these people whom I thought were my friends. Apparently I am not the person I perceived myself to be.

Mission Two is also a failure: no happy reunion with Bryan, Mason and Wendy.

Shakily I shell out from my pocket a generous estimate for what everyone has had—or eventually will have—this afternoon at Hamlet's. I put the money on a counter next to my ex-pals, so they can see this token of my fairness. Yet I'm aware that my actions are too late to fix the mistakes I apparently committed when I lived here among them. In less than four months I have become a living ghost, a less than pleasant memory.

I slurp my last through the straw. Getting up, I whisper "Goodbye," and can't think of anything else to add.

My three former friends nod and wave at me half-heartedly, someone mumbles "Later," and that's it. When you've completely lost yourself it's very taxing finding the strength to walk out the door.

WITH TWO STRIKES AGAINST ME, I have to go by subway as I attempt my third mission. This time I call ahead of time at the station, making sure I'm not barging in where I'm not wanted. Last chance to salvage something out of this messy trip.

HIS NEW HOUSE is even larger than the one they had up north. I learned on the telephone that Andy's parents are out for the day. No surprise there; I'm thankful nonetheless.

We're seated in his family room with the fireplace crackling, dwindling down.

He tries to smile, his face looks too weary to clinch it. Grinning slowly instead he says, "Look at you." Andy's voice fades. A haunting whisper, "Cynthia's boy."

I look right into those familiar gloomy eyes. "What's inside your head?" I ask.

He nods. "Let me guess what happened to you last night." Taking a deep even breath, he delivers an accurate summary of events. Basically he figures out there was a big wrestling event and that I was the one slated for torture, without my prior knowledge or consent.

Obviously he doesn't know the exact details. I have to fill him in on Sally and my dad, and the whole Mr. Kween weirdness. He ignores my dad's affair like it's a minor detail.

"And you think Renny the truck driver is this . . . Mr. Kween?"

"Yeah, haven't you heard what I said?"

"Jim, Renny's strange but I don't think he's the computer type."

"Who else could it be?"

He responds too quickly, "Me."

"Come on."

"Maybe it's somebody a thousand miles away. Who knows?"

I keep thinking it must be Renny. He was just pretending to be attracted to Lynda; the whole time he was interested in teenage boys. He has to be the one! However I realize I'm relying on wishful thinking so I won't have to accept the possibility that the culprit will always remain a mystery, just like a lot of other stuff in my lousy life. Putting both hands to the sides of my lowered head, relieved at least to be sitting down, I mutter, "I guess there's a million things I'll never know."

Andy sighs once more. "There are some things you should know, and I have to tell you them."

I crane up my head as my hands find my knees. "Is it going to be good news?"

He shakes his head unhappily. "But it's the truth."

ROCK TWENTY-ONE

A HUGE PINK AND PURPLE CLOUD outside the large window flows past the other side of Andy's head showing the dying of the day. Several shadow strands paint his dark profile. Poised in sadness, he has the mythical quality of some tragic literary character I've read about in English class. He makes no movement to put more logs into the fireplace where only faint embers glow.

"I didn't think you'd listen when I warned you about Cynthia," he begins.

"How did you know?"

"I knew her brother."

"Dan?" I ask.

"No, Tony. They're twins. Non-identical, though."

"Huh?"

"We used to hang out together. Tony would wrestle Dan, who was a lot smaller two years ago. You know, older brother beats up little brother?"

"Yeah." Cynthia has a male twin, and I have new-information overload!

Andy's calm tone unnerves me as he talks on. "He persuaded me to wrestle with him. Being so damn strong, Tony won every time but still it was fun. Something to do. He called himself Model T. That's how FRATS got started."

I give my head a shake. "Model T?" I don't want to rehash too much of what happened last night. "Cynthia's never once mentioned this other brother to me."

"Tony was wired. After the school expelled him, he became Fissure Rock's main drug supplier. Then he ripped off the wrong kind of people, and after some death threats, Mr. Sacalla (a pretty scary guy himself, as you know) said Tony would be safer living with him in Shift Creek."

"What do you mean, 'as I know'?"

Andy gives me a fatigued questioning look. "Who drove you half-way down here?"

One shock after another, and still I'm not immune to them. I take in a fast deep breath. "Renal . . . no! No way! Cynthia's father is Renaldo?"

"Bingo. Nobody's heard from Tony since. Maybe Mr. Sacalla killed him."

I don't want to mention that I actually met Model-T the night before. It would be too much for him in his present eerie state. So I simply suggest that Tony is probably involved in the backyard fed in Shift Creek. "I found out there's one up there."

"Interesting." He doesn't sound interested.

While I try to absorb it all Andy appears exhausted having told me these things, yet I know there's more coming. I wonder if the memories are too hard for him. Outside, the cloud has become dark grey. "Listen," I say, "let's save the rest of this talk for later. You look really bagged."

Rather than continuing staring into the fireplace, Andy's head slowly turns my way like an old elevator door opening lazily. "You don't understand," he whispers. His large brown eyes reveal large black pupils I never noticed before. "I have to tell you, and right away. What happened to you, it's my fault."

Everything's more difficult to see; the flames have almost flickered out. I'm hopelessly sliding into some kind of shadow land. "Andy, no way. Why are you blaming yourself?"

"Because I should have told you the whole truth that first day when I saw Cynthia . . . checking you out. I knew what she was up to." He says this with dread, like he's about to burst out crying. In a jittery voice, "Deep down I didn't want to warn you. I wanted to see what would happen to you. So I wouldn't be the only one."

There's a blip in my brain as I make a comparison: my jealousy of Dan's killer instinct. Yes, I can kind of understand what Andy is saying here. After I tell him, "I don't blame you for anything," he persists with his story.

"When Tony was running FRATS, he dreamed up the craziest storylines. We'd be sweating it out in his backyard on a hot summer day, him throwing me through more wooden boards than I could burn. It was just some wild fun, but then Cynthia talked privately with him and there'd be a stranger plot presented to me. You see, Cynthia wanted me . . . all to herself. Believe it or not, I didn't want that, but . . . we all like to be wanted, don't we? I really felt Tony was . . . an awesome friend. Anyway I did those things to please him (not her) and they're all on video."

Andy's talking slower than ever. It's an obvious extra effort for him to speak, period. I have to ask, "What things?"

He moves his head away from me so he can stare at the nearest darkened wall. "Cynthia had Tony stage these painful submission holds on me. After I submitted, gave up, cried uncle, whatever, she kept that damn camcorder recording. Maybe because I brushed off her come-ons, she paid me back with these heavy-duty close-ups; me in distress; my face sometimes covered in tears; the crotch of my shorts and . . . other things I don't want to talk about. Cynthia sells FRATS wrestling videos to whoever will pay for them. She even takes requests from her special highest-paying customers around the world and tries her best to satisfy them. Makes not bad money, either. Got the idea? You and me, we're both stars in the homes of perverts—such as this Mr. Kween of yours."

A sharp chill runs through my entire body. "She's crazy," I mumble.

"Yep," Andy sighs tiredly, "I knew that all along. Tony used to be different. She changed him."

"Hey," I say softly, "how can you change a person?"

His voice drawls on in the cold dark room. "Tony was special. You can't understand. There was a time he needed me because I helped him with his homework. When we talked, they were magical talks. Tony could be gentle. I miss him so." Suddenly he changes course, as if remembering only now I am in the room with him. "Sounds weird, doesn't it, two friends being so close? Cynthia sure didn't like it."

My feelings are raw scraped down to the bone. Aches and pains from last night return. Recalling his odd behaviour the first time I was at his swimming pool, I'm wondering if my former suspicions about Andy weren't true after all.

Andy is rambling on, a sputtering car on some remote coal-black road. "So I kept turning down her advances, and she absolutely hates it when people refuse her. Cynthia told Tony what she thought of our special friendship, and he changed all right. Lost all interest in school. Wouldn't let me help him study anymore. Everything between us dissolved into a routine of him doing these sadistic submission holds on me while Cynthia did the filming and enjoyed every painful second I endured. Oh, she revelled in her revenge. Even for Tony's sake, I couldn't tolerate this any longer. When he began pulverizing kids at school, he was beyond repair and got kicked out for it. I had to stay away from him. If only she never got in the way."

I sit there unmovable, everything in the open; why he held such hostility for Cynthia right from the start. "What made her be like this?" I whimper.

"I heard Mr. Sacalla was brutal to her mother when they were married—a real mean drunk. Weird thing is, after they got divorced, he was the one who gave up alcohol. Mrs. Sacalla gave Cynthia and Dan strict instructions never to acknowledge Renny as their father, to treat him like something invisible—so he treated them the same way. Who knows why we turn out the way we do?"

There's too much stillness in here. The darkness keeps closing in, making me feel very claustrophobic. Andy's breathing is funny (as in not humorous), lots of weak gasps for air, and I wonder if he's crying. I don't know what more to say, so I don't say anything.

"You never asked me how I've been since I moved to the big city," he sighs quietly.

He's right. I should have asked. Why can't I say what people expect me to? Why does it always have to be about me? I'm way too self-absorbed. "Sorry, I want to know. Please tell me."

"I'm failing all my courses. My parents are warning me they'll send me back to the orphanage, except I know I'm too old—"

"Orphanage?" I repeat.

"I'm adopted. They like to use it as leverage."

I clearly remember Mr. and Mrs. Bradford. It's hard to forget parents like that. I swing back to the subject of his grades, "You were a top student at Fissure Rock."

"Yeah, almost gave Cynthia a run for top banana on the honour roll. Who knew she'd replace Tony as the town's sole drug supplier, using Joe as her decoy? FRATS videos are secondary for her. They come in handy when the hallucinogens run dry. The drugs, that's where the big money comes from. She's got a monopoly up there."

Maybe I should be shocked by this news, but nothing can jolt me at this point. In early evening blackness Andy breathes his words out, slurring many of them. Bizarre, but I listen to his slow motion recounting with something akin to morbid fascination. I'm not sure why I get this feeling.

"Believe it or not I used to have some friends there in old FR. Cynthia made sure I was totally isolated after she found out what was going on between me and . . ." He pauses. "I mean, you just don't quit FRATS. You must know, between her and her mother, they own Fissure Rock. My folks got fed up with the prank phone calls . . . things anonymous kids were saying about me—even though many were true—it doesn't matter now. Finally we moved down to this fine city of yours. Kind of ironic, isn't it? The place your family moved away from?"

Andy stops for a moment to balance his wobbly breathing, then resumes, "Actually you're the last person I wanted to see."

Now I feel more terrible than ever. "I know, I know. I apologize for calling you up out of the blue."

It's far too dark to see. In my mind I can picture his calm deer-like eyes and his head shaking reverently, as he says blindly, "No, you don't get it."

"All I get," I begin with newly-formed determination, "is that Cynthia owes us both big-time for all this crap she's pulled!"

"Jim, you have no idea how much I miss you. Since I first saw you sitting there in Mr. King's English class, you've been in my dreams." Andy clicks on a lamp and lightning splits me in half. Looking at him, the palest face I've ever seen stares back at me. As white as that snow outside.

He must be ill, I tell myself.

"I'm so happy you called before you came over," he insists with very little strength left. "You're the last person I'm going to see. That's the way I . . . wanted it to be . . . ."

His eyes roll back with his head, his body goes limp in the chair.

Standing up I shout, "Andy! Wake up! What's going on?"

His eyelids barely open as he slurs one last time, "When mother gets home, she's going to be most upset with me. Due to my inconsiderate actions, she'll need to refill the prescription for her sleeping pills." Andy's slow narrative comes to a halt. Unconsciousness overtakes him.

"WHAT?"

ROCK TWENTY-TWO

WOULDN'T YOU KNOW IT? After I call 9-1-1, and look at Andy again, nature calls me. My bladder's bursting. What are you supposed to do in this situation? First I check his pulse. It's weak and slow, but he's got one. Pacing the floor for hour-long seconds, I finally figure if you've got to go, you've got to go. Zipping into the washroom I unzip.

While relieving myself, I try to drain the guilt inside me. Feeling tears well up in my eyes and my throat getting sore, I swallow hard, clench my teeth together and flex my face muscles into a determined frown. I'm forcing myself not to care anymore about anything or anyone. It hurts too much! If Andy wants to die, let him. He's made his decision, he talked about it enough before, and I won't be held responsible. The ambulance and police people arrive just as I'm washing my hands.

As I near the family room (weird name for it in Andy's household), the ambulance woman and guy busily strap him into a stretcher. The police hurl a million questions my way: Who am I? What happened? What's his name? Where are his parents? Answering them as best I can, their faces cast identically contemptuous expressions when my reply to "Where were you just now?" is "I had to take a leak." I'm just too composed for their liking, I guess. But remember, I've resolved not to care.

With the woman at the wheel, and me inside for the ride, the ambulance coasts to the hospital. They're really in no rush. A routine pick-up, it seems, and I wonder who cares less, them or me? Andy looks peaceful sleeping there as the male attendant tries to get him awake, lightly slapping his face. I sit there and think how none of this matters. Not intending to be callous, I'm asking myself why do we all go to such great lengths to stay alive, and keep sick people alive, and keep people who want to die alive, when we're all going to die anyway? What's the deal? We aren't worth shit, none of us.

Maybe I'm in shock. The shrill siren and whirling red light slicing into the night don't bother me one iota. All the sound and fury in the world can't do anything to me. In fact it's almost funny: a slow-moving ambulance making so much noise. I'm way past feeling. Been there, done that. To test this new persona I've adopted, I look at my watch. My hand is not shaking. The time is perfectly clear: 8:00 p.m.

This attendant, who's now sort of pinching Andy's face, speaks calmly. "Hey kid, open up those lids of yours, okay? Work with me." (So people actually do say that.)

Andy doesn't appear ready to cooperate. Perhaps he detects the apathy in the man's tone. He just wants to sleep . . . sleep . . . die.

Practically bored, the man with the big curly black moustache talks on, "Andy, time to wake up, guy."

I wonder how much longer I can hide. I've got to be honest, my heart is racing and I feel as if I am dying alongside Andy. Why don't these two ambulance people simply take both him and me to the nearest graveyard, throw us into an open hole, and fill it in with dirt? There is nothing to live for; it hurts to know this truth. That's how I'm really feeling, while I continue pretending not to feel at all.

ONE HOUR IS SPENT WAITING in the hospital emergency room, and it's a long hour. Someone in authority then comes out to tell me the good news. They've successfully pumped Andy's stomach. He'll be fine. His parents have been notified and are on their way. I'm heralded as a brave and loyal friend to have done what I did. What did I do? I'm invited to see him; I decline. This is the way it should end between Andy and me. Thinking of those things he said back at his house, well, it would be too embarrassing . . . for Andy, I mean.

"I have to go home," I say to the unknown authority, and into the cold night I go.

BACK ON THE SUBWAY and in a flash I am at my city starting point.

WALKING ALONG SNOW-BANKED STREETS to face the Ganderworts, and Sideline (my feline friend who has forsaken me), I see someone's beloved five-year-old Malibu in the driveway. This hasn't been my luckiest day! Sooner or later, my parents would come to find me. I'm going to have to decide which one I want to live with since their marriage has been smashed to smithereens. Considering all that's happened, returning to Fissure Rock would be as strange as trying to stay here in the city. I feel like there's no place for me. I further gather that Mrs. Ganderwort phoned my folks, after making certain I'd come back, and told them where I would be. She's a clever one.

Mrs. G ushers me in.

Mom isn't here.

Dad and I hold this long serious stare and we can't seem to read each other's mind. I'm still trying my hardest not to feel anything, like I'm frostbitten, but I sure am mad at him. He looks older than I've ever seen him, with his salt-and-pepper hair kind of messed-up and those few wrinkles on his face suddenly ultra-magnified.

Just when I think nothing is going to break our gaze, Mr. Ganderwort surprises all of us, "I told you both before! I don't want the newspaper delivered anymore!"

Mrs. G lovingly pats her husband on the shoulder. "Now, now, Jules. You musn't upset yourself, dear. These aren't the newspaper people." She's so gentle with him, and she gets the old guy to sit quietly on the sofa with her.

Dad and I keep standing, looking solemnly at each other, neither one knowing what to say. We can hear each other's restrained breathing.

Then he says calmly, "Get your backpack and let's go home."

"I came to get Sideline."

He keeps his eyes right on mine. "The cat belongs to the Ganderworts now."

"He was my cat."

We're like two cowboys at a high-noon duel in an old western TV movie.

"Jim, I don't intend to argue—"

"Me neither." He thinks I'm going to flinch under his stare. Better think again, Pops!

"Son, the Ganderworts need the cat more than you do. It's a good companion for them at their stage in life. You're only sixteen, you don't—"

"Thanks, I know how old I am. You always hated Sideline."

"When did I say that, Jim?"

And now I've started feeling again. Bad, that is. Dad's just asked a good question, even if it is skirting the issue, and I haven't got an answer.

To break the tension, Mrs. G pipes up, "Bill, I believe it would be best if Jim took his cat back with him."

I'm relieved she didn't call my cat Snowbell again. Still looking fiercely into Dad's eyes I almost whisper, "Thanks, Mrs. G."

My father turns his head away from me to look at the old couple on the couch. "Only if you're absolutely certain, Elizabeth."

Our stare-down is over and I win. Big deal.

She laughs and stands up. "Oh, Jules isn't fussy about cats anyway."

What she's just said has got to be the understatement of the year. Her husband probably doesn't even know there's a cat in here . . . what a cat is . . . where here is . . . or who he is!

"I'll get his cage for you," Mrs. G says as she scurries from the room. Some old people never get old. She's the complete opposite of her husband.

Looking back at me Dad asks, "You okay?"

Before I can think of a good comeback Mr. Ganderwort mumbles, "I'm just fine, thank you."

Everybody's a liar.

ROCK TWENTY-THREE

WE'RE IN THE CAR AND BUCKLED UP. Sideline's meowing malicious protests from inside his cage, which rests on my lap. My pet doesn't realize I am rescuing, not cat-napping, him. Dad hangs onto a thought for a long moment. The car engine remains unstarted. At first I'm waiting for all the predictable questions, followed by maybe a lecture, to pour out of him. What he does instead is absolutely unexpected, out of character. Quickly his whole arm swings toward me and I can't duck out of the way in time. He's got it wrapped around my shoulders, embracing me tightly.

Time passes and I'm beyond uncomfortable. In a quavering voice he says, "I'm so thankful you're all right."

My God, I think he's on the edge of tear-duct land. What a crocodile!

Letting go of me, he starts the car and it crawls along city streets until we hit the nearest ramp that winds around like a coiling tentacle. Then he floods the pedal to get the Malibu onto the highway like the rest of the monkeys behind their steering wheels. Everyone's going nowhere fast on this black winter night called life.

"Why did you do that?" I ask.

"Hmm?"

"What's up with the big hug back there?"

Watching the highway like an eagle, his eyes blink rapidly three times, and he swallows hard. A weak voice answers, "Something my own father never did for me. He ran out of time, I suppose." That's all he can manage, so he refocuses on his driving while biting his lower lip.

And that's the last thing I remember before falling asleep.

IT TURNS OUT TO BE a dull dreamless four-hour slumber, exactly what I need.

DAD TOUSLES MY HAIR with his palm and long fingers. "Hey, wake up."

Groaning, I open my eyes. Here we are, parked in the driveway of 4 Ducksback Drive, back in this insane little town. My dad acts like nothing's amiss, though he does seem slightly more solemn than usual. I close my eyes again as he opens his door to get out. A rush of freezing air makes me think that Andy had the right idea. Playing this game of lies called life is really taking its toll on me. Why can't I just die?

Dad has reached the passenger door and pries it open. "Come on, Jim. You're too big to carry. Shake a leg."

I sense Sideline, trapped in his cage, taken off my lap. Slowly I place my right foot out onto the driveway. My injuries throb. Reopening my eyes, I see Mom sniffling as she looks at me from inside the front screen door. Lisa is right behind her wearing a serious expression. Hauling myself out of the car and exhaling a cloud into the chilly black air, I teeter. If not for Dad, I'd be flat on the asphalt. But his free arm is around my shoulders once again, and it guides me to where I don't want to go. There are issues in our house that I simply wish to avoid.

SIDELINE HISSES AT ALL FOUR OF US as my father lowers the cage to the floor. We take off our coats and footwear in the front hall. Mom dabs at her eyes with a tissue, then bends down and presses on the little clip that opens my cat's prison.

Sideline has always been extremely smart. He immediately guns for safer quarters underneath the sofa. Wish I could do the same thing as Mom gives me yet another hug, which is (this time, coming from her, at a time like this) perfectly predictable.

My body is never going to get a chance to heal. And something's missing from this sad scene: words.

Lisa helps break the icy tension. "I see Sideline's still a suck." There's no energy in her remark. It's more a trivial aside. Someone else is imitating my sister.

Mom gives her a look that only the two of them would know anything about. Lisa goes into the kitchen to make tea. I'd heard the kettle whistling as soon as I walked through the doorway, as surely as the siren of the ambulance where Andy was strapped up inside. The sound begins to grate on my nerves. I'm thawing out. If ever I thought I was tough, and for awhile back there I believed so, that time is over. Feelings are jumping back at me in an approaching tidal wave starting in the horizon. I'm like a little boy who has done something bad. No, it can't be. I'm not the perpetrator in all this mess; I'm the victim. Me!

Soon Mom and Dad are standing awkwardly with me in the living room. She says, "We're all going to sit down and talk everything out."

Ah, a family meeting. We've never had one of those before.

When Lisa returns with the tea tray, I note that everyone is bleary-eyed save for me. Of course it is two-thirty in the morning, and I already had a long nap in the car.

Dad takes charge of things in his smooth, underhanded manner. "Jim, we have news for you."

Oh, the dramatic pause of it all. This is like some B-rated movie, or a soap opera. I'm completely aware of what my parents are going to say, prior to them voicing anything. When was the last time someone in my family said anything that could be classified as news? After everything I've gone through today, never mind last night, do they really expect to surprise me?

I'll admit I might be fuzzy on their precise words ahead of time but certain of the gist of it. First they'll tell me how overjoyed they are that I'm safe, and how ever so worried they were regarding my whereabouts all day. Second there'll be a confirmation of Lisa's omen: a divorce is pending and things must be discussed, custody and all that. What else? Dad will apologize profusely to everyone for his wrong-doings and plead for forgiveness. Mom might cry again, causing Lisa to sigh and roll her eyes in utter disgust. Yeah, I imagine I've summed it up pretty well in my head. I'm prepared.

Interesting how we're all seated far apart from each other. Lisa's in her favourite chair. Mom's got the wooden rocker, thanks to having had the winning ticket at the Fissure Rock Horse Fair last month. Dad has chosen the left side of the sofa, and I am four feet away from him on the right side, directly above where Sideline is hiding out. Actually it's not so interesting, this predictable arrangement.

"Son," Dad starts once more, "your mother and I . . . we've both been far too lenient with you."

What? My eyes enlarge. Talk about new directions.

"You are unbelievably stubborn," adds Mom with a disapproving slowly shaking head, "and selfish. We're extremely disappointed in you."

Bang! There go my aspirations in clairvoyance as a career, shot out of the sky. I just can't get anything right, lately. Damn!

Dad sugars his tea and stirs. "What were you hoping to gain by running away like that? And we want an honest answer, Jim. None of this going back to get Sideline business."

I think, and I think, and I think. But I still don't know if I am. "I thought . . . after what Lisa said . . ." I stop and look at Lisa. She switches her gaze to the hardwood floor. Sideline, hidden, meows helplessly.

"I see," says my mother less vexed, "Lisa's told you."

"No," my sister lies.

"Yes," I say truthfully. What is she trying to pull this time?

My once revered father steps into the fray. "All right, so why would that cause you to suddenly take off?"

Mom pours it on, not giving me a chance to respond to Dad. "Your face is a mess! Lisa told us about this . . . this despicable wrestling nonsense! That is going to end as of now! And that Cynthia girl is also history. Understood?" She sips from her steaming teacup. Quite a masterful performance! Should I salute?

Instead I nod. Hey, I wouldn't dream of protesting on either count.

"Your mother and I care about you, Jim. Don't ever forget that." Dad's getting lovey-dovey. "We were troubled about your low marks in Math and Science, and now this. Your good judgment is slipping. I used to be able to count on you, pal."

I've reached my limit. Cracking apart inside and out I shout, "What a load of crap!"

All eyes turn, firing on me. I see my sister's are the widest—and most worried.

"What about you?" I scream at Dad. "Having an affair with your boss!"

Lisa whispers, "Jimmy, shut up."

"James Oliver Bridgeman!" my mother enunciates with solid parental authority.

"Oh, give it a break, Mom, I'm not five anymore! Lisa's already told me everything."

"Jimmy, stop it!" Lisa bellows.

I don't take orders from her. "What about that drunk-fest with Sally Sacalla last night, Dad? Huh? Care to explain?"

My good-old dad inhales with great consideration, and slowly lets his breath out. He's quiet and composed. "Now I'm not so sure what Lisa did tell you."

He sends a look her way, and to my amazement she turns her head away in . . . fear? Shame? Lisa?

Back to me he speaks, "I wasn't drinking, Jim. But you're certainly right about Sally's condition. She smashed up her car and I was with her. Neither one of us were hurt, in case you care."

Mom looks at me, her mouth wide open, and now I feel guilty again.

How many wrong turns am I allowed in this game? "You mean Sally and you aren't . . . ?"

Dad's miffed. "Well you didn't have any trouble saying it before, son." Prolonged cumbersome pause. "No, we're not having an affair."

I don't believe him. "Mom? You're accepting all this?"

She's firm with her reply, "Your father has never lied to anyone in this family. I would know if he said something that wasn't true."

I glance at my father and I feel stupid. He decides to further satisfy my curiosity. "Yes, Sally had been flirting with me for a long time. I didn't read it right. Last night I realized it wasn't all harmless fun, that she was serious. I told her: no way. She got very upset, and after some nasty words to me she ended up crashing into that tree."

Suddenly, I wonder what kind of tree "that tree" is. I don't understand why my brain works the way it does; it does get me in trouble sometimes.

Mom carries on. "Every night your father came home from working late, he gave me the details about Sally's behaviour towards him. We discussed whether or not it was simply her way of being friendly or silly, and if he should quit. There were many things at stake; you and Lisa, for example. Bills have to be paid. And now everything about her intentions is crystal clear."

Fine, I'm not the only one who's been going through a lot lately, and I'm also not the only one who has made mistakes. Mom should be targeting Lisa at this point. It was she who got it all wrong about Sally and Dad. As a minimal show of fairness or something, she ought to be accosted for jumping to conclusions. Come on, why am I taking all the heat? But, no, both my parents seem to be giving her major slack, treating her like some rare tropical plant that might die if you even breathe around it too hard. Lisa?

Dad says to my sister, "I think it's time you told your brother the real news, honey." Honey?

I hear Sideline, in vain, let out another pitiful meow.

"Jim?" For once she calls out my name in one syllable, and her voice is faint, "I'm pregnant."

ROCK TWENTY-FOUR

NEXT DAY COMES SOON ENOUGH and way too early, even though it's almost noon when I awake. Half of me tries sorting out all this news, logically; the other half deals with the continued return of my feelings—like a furnace, grumbling at first and getting warmer, but not yet hot. On my side in bed, very alone, I ruminate.

How could Lisa, taking into account her misanthropic tendencies and all, let (or get) any Fissure Rock guy to go that far with her? Last night, though, she told us the name of the boy responsible. I couldn't believe it when she said it. Gerald's innocent face and timid mannerisms had definitely concealed some major desires. His responsibility was planted the day before our family's departure for this lowdown town. Everything is much clearer now. Lisa's time on the internet was mostly spent chatting with Gerald; her switching preference for baggier clothes and her increased eating habits were both attempts to make her body appear larger overall, averting our eyes from what her stomach would grow into—a pathetic attempt, stalling for time.

It wasn't merely a case of Lisa missing Gerald causing her to be so bitchy all the time. She knew all along that part of him was inside her. His part won't be staying there, though. Mom and Dad agreed that a trip back to the city is necessary for a quiet operation. Since certain Fissure Rock folks are holier-than-whatever, if news escapes about Lisa being pregnant, well, that'd be bad enough. However my family would be finished in this town if information leaked out about her having an abortion. Call it telepathy if you want, but I also know Lisa secretly wants to have Gerald's baby. She's broken-hearted, powerless to even suggest something different than what my parents have already planned, and I share her pain. If only none of this had ever happened.

When will all these horrible and sad events end? Hamlet comes to my mind again, his heavy words: "How weary, stale, flat and unprofitable seem to me all the uses of this world! Fie on it, ah fie. 'Tis an unweeded garden that grows to seed. Things rank and gross in nature possess it merely."

As much as I hate the prospect of staying here, I know I must remain and slay the dragons in my path. I guess you could say vengeance is on my mind, but I think that's reasonable. I'm also thinking about those sessions Cynthia and I had going for a while. We made it to third base (if that's what it's called) several times; we never went all the way. Sounds awful, yeah, I'm kind of jealous of my little sister and Gerald. Here I am, still a virgin, and Lisa's got undeniable proof that she's not. Wait, what is this, a friggin' competition? Time for me to get up.

DOWNSTAIRS. Peeking outside the window above the kitchen sink, I spot snow transforming into sinister shapes. Silver pipes of slippery ice grip the backyard fence. Glancing upwards, my eyes are impaled on a sad grey sky. I scan the room for my family, and we mumble subdued and dutiful morning acknowledgements at one another. Then, catching my reflection in the kettle on the stove, illusion blends into reality: I am far away and distorted. None of us have taken time to worry about our appearances today. We're like a group of refugees dragging ourselves away from some brutal war battle zone. There's nothing for us to say. Ironically, Santa Claus will soon be coming to town.

WE SOMEHOW EXCHANGE PRESENTS on Christmas Day, knowing full well that two days later my parents and Lisa will be travelling to the city to stay overnight while she has her delicate operation. I don't remember or care about what gifts I give or get.

We're all walking zombies. And I wish there was something, anything, I could do for my sister.

I HOLD OFF until the three of them are dressed in the front hall and the car is warming up in the driveway. Finally I ask my dad, "How are we going to keep living here? I mean, after everything that's gone on."

He tells me, "That's life, son." No longer are his words those of a never-say-die dreamer; it appears reality's sunk in to stay for all of us.

"Besides," my mother pitches in, "if we sold this house in today's market, we'd never get the money we need to move someplace else. We're not rich."

('Wow, there's news! Thanks for the mundane information, Mom. Have a nice trip. Bye!')

Really I expected their answers. I've resolved, as they prepare to leave, that I will attend to a certain matter in their absence. They both ask if I'll be okay on my own. I answer very positively. Get this, I give Lisa a hug and she allows me this show of affection. No show; it's heartfelt.

They're gone.

I know my remedy.

SWEET AS A BUTTER-TART on the phone, I jokingly explain that my keepers are away for the whole night and she should come on over, alone. There is hesitation on her part as she calculates the humour and lightness in my tone, inquires how I'm feeling and tries to pump me for my take on what went on at Splinter Wonderland, as if she didn't know! But I don't give her any hints about me having been hurt by Dan, or my travelling anywhere, or finding out anything from Andy. She has no idea what's in store. For once, she will experience what it's like when the tables are turned on her. There is absolutely no escape for Cynthia Sacalla.

SHE RINGS MY DOORBELL late in the afternoon while the sun is setting—how fitting. After I let her in and hang up her coat, we kiss and embrace, small talk, our usual prelude. Suddenly I note the navy blue corduroy skirt and silky white blouse underneath her pink crochet sweater. And perfume. Are we off to the opera? She is an enticing sight. My pulsing signal of resolve prior to her arrival is now encountering severe static. I knew this would happen; I must firm up.

We sit in the living room: me in an armchair and her, opposite, on the sofa. I suggest we have a pizza delivered for dinner, and she's fine with that.

I don't order just yet. Time for my verbal appetizer. "By the way," I begin my cavalier performance, "how do you like my new face?" Mind you it's beginning to heal fine, but still stands out in a pale yellowish shade.

"Oh, Jim!" her voice rains compassion. "I was waiting for you to tell me; I didn't want to pry." Her eyes try to lock into mine. "How did you do that?" Yes, she's all concern, following my mention of the fact.

With Cynthia I know I have to play my cards very carefully. Putting it mildly, this girl's crafty. Tonight, though, she's met her match.

Laughter spills from me. Everything's pre-planned and under control, my control. Then I stop laughing. My answer to her is carefree, "No, no, I didn't do it. Your brother saved me the trouble." My put-on smile feels plastered there.

Her eyes shift to and fro; she's momentarily unaware of which game I'm playing. "Not at Splinter Wonderland!" She looks up at me with shock stuck in her cold blue eyes, the same peepers I'd previously misread for empathy and romance.

"Yeah, it's too bad you had to take care of . . . other things. I'm sure if you were there, you would have had a handle on the whole show." I'm baiting her.

"I just can't believe what Danny does sometimes! I'll talk to him, don't you worry." Very convincing; she might want to consider an acting career.

Enraged I am. "You're just guessing it was Dan who did this? Nope, I think you've known from the beginning. It's all on video. You've probably reviewed it already. You're in charge of everything involving FRATS. I know all about you!"

Smiling, she flutters her eyelashes like a southern belle. "Please say it isn't so." Cynthia hasn't exactly avoided my hook. Rather she's grabbed my rod and is pulling with all her might, downright mocking me. Got to give her credit, she's Fissure Rock's brightest bitch.

This isn't going to be easy, but I'm determined to rock her. "Knock it off, Cynthia, will you?"

"Jim," she sighs, "why do you have to be so melodramatic all the time? You're beginning to bore me."

I pause, wondering who she is. Who is she, really? I can't help myself as I ask, "What are you up to?"

"Hmm," she pretends to think hard, maintaining a mischievous grin. Her hands fold underneath her chin. "I was under the impression that you were about to tell me." Cynthia crosses her feet at the ankles on top of the coffee table in front of her. She spreads out her arms, crucifix-fashion, palms down on top of the sofa.

Christ, I hadn't counted on such a blasé reaction. I've played some tennis in my time, but this strategy of hers is something else. (Out of nowhere, I suddenly remember a school project I once presented on one of the most famous tennis matches in Wimbeldon's history. It was John McEnroe versus Bjorn Borg, and Borg kept the title for a fifth consecutive year. Afterwards the defeated McEnroe said to reporters: 'I was playing tennis; I don't what he was playing.')

"Or," Cynthia goes on, "do you want to order the pizza first? To be honest I'm getting kind of hungry."

I stare at her, my mouth wide open. This is unreal. I'm thinking of Dan's relentless hunger to inflict pain on others; of Tony's shady past as school bully and community drug lord; of

Sally and her sneaky plan to snare my father away from us. This time I can picture Renaldo as having once been part of this family of hers. It does seem to click together. Sickened by my memories and images, I let out with something else. "Look, I took a trip to visit Andy a few days ago."

"Did you?" She perks right up. "How is he?" Cynthia's teeth shine too brightly.

"Like you care," I whisper.

Her expression is inscrutable. She doesn't respond.

"I found out about the custom-made wrestling videos for those special customers around the globe, about who Tony is, about the drug money you rake in." I have to take a breath. A flood of further bad feelings flow through me. "Should I go on?" My armpits are wet. Talk about nerve-racking situations.

For a flash of eternity I sense something displace inside her. I'm not sure what, or even how to explain it. I just know it's like a trace of a substance—an emotion deep within her, perhaps, that almost bubbles out—and it disappears in a fraction of a second. Is there something there I can trip up? Can I summon it to the surface and watch it gush forth? Her silence continues.

"Well?" I wait for her to say something.

"Jim, what exactly is your problem?"

Once again I'm unable to rattle her. "Didn't you hear a word I said?"

Cynthia nods. "Yes, every one."

"I was hoping you'd deny it, at least."

"Would you believe me?" There's no sign of guilt anywhere on her face.

"Am I wrong?" (I know I'm not.)

She challenges me. "Why is this so important to you?" And her face is calm in its confusion.

My entire plan crumbles to the ground as if an earthquake has ripped through me. "The way you come across to everyone, I believed your reputation was . . . spotless! I thought you were . . . as close to perfect as perfect could be." Like a bull in a china shop, I add these words, "That's why I fell in love with you."

"Jim, get real," she says, almost playfully. "Now, who's denying things?"

"What am I denying?"

"That you want to screw me." She says this like she's talking about a tomcat instead of a human being. "I mean, who puts these mushy fairy tales into your feathery little brain? No wait, I know, it's your mother. Correct?" I can't accept this is her talking. It's not like her, not how I'd pictured her all along.

Instinctively I retaliate with whatever I can find. "At least I'm not a drug supplier. What if somebody blows the whistle on you someday? You want to go to jail?"

She smiles again. "Now don't you agree that Joe would make a much more suitable candidate for a jail cell than me?"

I shake my head with so much force I get a little dizzy. Then again, maybe it's just this whole surreal scene.

Cynthia speaks again, "Better take a close look at yourself, Jim. I believe it was you who was extremely stoned at the bonfire."

I offer a weak defence. "Well, I've hardly smoked the stuff since."

"Well I've never smoked it, period. It would simply get in the way."

I'm aghast. I try putting my point into business terms so she can understand. "You provide the product."

She comes right back at me. "A healthy portion from the video sales goes towards the charitable goals that Mrs. Kishwar and the entire town are very happy I help them to reach. I am preparing financially for my future and building a solid academic record for myself. I'll leave FRH, go on to university and eventually succeed in the business of my choice. I plan to see this world and grab everything I can get from life. I have too much potential to waste. Is there something wrong with any of this?"

Looking into her obstinate face, through those wild blue eyes, I realize that she just can't see. She looks at the forest only to lose sight of the trees. It may be hopeless, yet on I march. "So you don't care who gets hurt?"

Cynthia seems worn out, like I'm an unruly child with whom

she is entrusted. "I satisfy a demand and Joe is quite happy with his percentage, too. Who am I hurting?"

Quick answer from me: "Andy, for starters."

Unexpectedly she scowls. I've tripped her up and she stumbles, "Try the other way around."

"How did Andy hurt you, Cynthia?"

"Never mind. You're not allowed to know everything about me." Ice cold.

"You're just too afraid to tell me."

"Oh, please," she moans defiantly. Pursing her lips like an angry old lady, she spouts out: "I am afraid of nothing!"

"Fine," I press on. "What could Andy have possibly done to harm you?"

She looks genuinely sad, as I catch her still off guard. "He broke my heart." Apparently at one time Cynthia had a heart and it was capable of being broken.

"How?"

Quietly she offers a few fragmented phrases of explanation. "Tony and him . . . I didn't know that Andy was . . . he never said." She checks herself and stops.

I ask her in all seriousness, "Is that really Andy's fault?"

"I loved him." Apparently she was also once vulnerable enough to be in love.

"What about me, Cynthia? Did you ever love me?" In anticipation, I freeze.

She switches topic like some talented basketball player skilfully changing direction during the big game. There's a return to her cheery self. "You're a great guy, Jim! As long as you keep certain things to yourself, Joe won't have to risk going to jail and everything will be fine. Why don't you order the pizza now and later we'll make out." She tacks on, "You can go as far as you want with me, tonight. You've earned it." Striking me full force is her trademark public relations shining face.

This time I've figured it out. "If you thought there'd be any chance of me saying yes, after all this, you wouldn't have just made that offer."

Cynthia's seething. I detect a definite dint in her armour. "Like I said before, Jim, you're undeniably aching for me. You can't hide it. Start taking advantage of opportunities while they're still available! Why are you delaying?"

"You said you loved Andy, but you can't say the same thing about me."

She stands up quickly, thrusts her fists into the air and shakes them in frustration. "Oh, don't get love mixed up in it! We're wasting precious time! Do you know how much fun we could be having right now? And I did not say I loved Andy! Never!"

Likewise I get to my feet and say, "I don't get it. When you said—"

Closing her eyes she quietly informs me, "I was talking about Tony."

"This doesn't make sense. You loved Andy, but because he—"

"No. Andy got between Tony and me, and I won't ever forgive him for that."

My throat closes in on me. So Andy didn't realize what she was really mad about, he didn't know this. He thought she was coming on to him, but . . . this latest news is making me almost physically ill. "You mean you and your twin brother—?"

Cynthia winces. "Tony, my twin? He's my stepbrother."

I think, and I think, and I think. Okay, so Andy had made another wrong assumption. "But still, that's like—"

"You know what, Jim? I'm leaving. You're cute, very cute, but that's not enough in my books. You've accused me of the most disgusting things, and I refuse to be judged by someone who hasn't got a clue about where he's headed in life. Really I thought you were different, but there are too many apron strings tied around you. I can't believe how naïve you are. No offence, but you're just not sophisticated enough for me."

She gets up, grabs her coat and hat from the front hall closet and closes the door behind her with authority.

ROCK TWENTY-FIVE

EVEN AFTER MY PARENTS AND LISA RETURN nothing gets back to normal. What is normal? The word sounds strange. Dad concentrates on beginning his own advertising business, Mom is working more hours at the library and a very depressed Lisa sleeps a lot. The New Year is nearly here and, soon on its heels, another school semester will kick in.

I STAY AWAY FROM Lynda's Home Cooking, not wishing to run into Renaldo Sacalla again. There is no place in this town that I wish to go to anymore.

I STRUM AT DARK MINOR CHORDS on my guitar and write them down in case of memory breakdown (closer to nervous breakdown, feels like). The new song I'm working on? My ordeal here at good old Fissure Rock. Lyrics are hard to come by this time. Emotionally it's still too close, I guess. My music is fast and angry, though. I've already got a title: 'Broken Desire.'

I ACTUALLY HAD a long talk with my father, gave him the rundown on Cynthia, Dan and FRATS (the very much-edited version of all three). Extraneous detail would not be healthy for him at this point—stressful enough starting up a new business. He gave me practical advice. "Forget them and move on," he said. "Be proactive, son. Anyone can be a follower, or a critic. If she's anything like her mother . . . Well, you simply can't change people, that's for sure. Work on improving your own weaknesses."

Taking this as a further attack on me, I got my back up again. "I know, I know! I have to focus on my studying, get better grades . . ."

"I'm not preaching at you, Jim." He remained perfectly peaceful and friendly, helpful. "I have faults that I'm mending, too. It helps me when I set a goal and work towards it. Now you can take what I'm saying whichever way you choose."

And I know he's right; how can he not be? Yes, better to be happy than sad. Bypass the bad stuff. I know, I know. Still it's hard. Awkward feelings always brush up against my good reasoning. The end result is a chaotic clash.

Don't you think I'd love to be a natural born leader, such as you-know-who, and strut my way through life like a winner? Part of me yearns to be a mover and shaker, instead of fumbling among the moved and shaken. Yet I keep thinking about people I'd be hurting in the process. Who gets left behind, trampled on, enabling me to charge ahead? I mean if somebody wins, then somebody loses. 'Guilty' remains my middle name. Maybe I have to face facts: I'm a loser because I lack the balls to be otherwise.

DAYS WHIP BY. Our family mourns in the New Year. Another school term commences, and it proves to be the end for me. Invisible is how I'm treated within and without the hallowed halls of FRH. No one looks at me, nobody. Even Joe walks right by me without a word. My feelings for Cynthia are defiled. Sure a physical desire for her lingers, you bet. But implanted deep inside my brain is a new feeling more distasteful than hate. It festers like a sharp wooden sliver dulled with time. (I know all about sharp wooden slivers.)

MY STOMACH NO LONGER DIGESTS FOOD very well, and I'm often not hungry enough to eat anything. Some days I feel like I can't take in a deep breath. Other times my heart doesn't beat right; it stumbles, skips, and does triple trembles. Especially after falling asleep, I wake up scared that I'm about to die. My folks even raced me to the hospital one night, but a check of all vital signs satisfied the doctor that I was simply suffering from anxiety. "Relax" was the only prescription he gave me. That's when my parents hinted that I should see a psychiatrist. No way, I'm not the one who's crazy!

I KEEP REPEATING TO MYSELF over and over, like a mantra, "Forget them." Dad knows best. The most productive way is to use their silent treatment to my advantage: work damn hard at my schoolwork. But nothing I try works for long. It's as if I'm drowning.

EVEN SIDELINE SPENDS more time with everybody else in my family than he does with me. How pathetic is that?

IT'S A SUNDAY MORNING and Lisa's noiselessly watching TV downstairs. I wonder if I should go down to talk with her. How would I begin the conversation? What are the right words?

Using our computer in her bedroom, I use internet messenger to type to Andy: 'How's everything going? I hope you're okay. How could I be so stupid? Now I know what it must have felt like for you when you were up here—almost, at least. I'm sorry about everything.'

Whether or not I'm shell-shocked, Andy's nearly instantaneous reply mildly jolts me: 'Hi! On-line almost all the time, before and after school, on weekends; meeting all kinds of new people. Even my parents have been giving me a lot less stress since, well, you know. Anyway Jim, it's good to hear (read?) from you. I'm chatting with some really cool guys right now. Don't be sorry, be happy, and thanks for helping me. If it wasn't for you I wouldn't be here. You're a great friend. Keep in touch. Later.'

Robotically I close down all programs, disconnect from the internet and switch off the computer. Andy's moving on with his life; he's forgiven me, even thanked me. Why can't I let go of my troubles? I'm a nobody at FRH again. So what? I've been in this lonely spot before, when we first moved here.

This isn't the way it should end!
Heinous crimes been committed!
There has to be a payback!
Revenge!
Justice.
Something?

I'm back alone in my room. Grabbing paper and pen I start cutting the words for my new song. Like a wild spreading fire, my boiling blood and searing sweat smear across the sheet in rhyme. Next, I grab my guitar and my pick. The chords I'd already thrashed together a couple of weeks before resound as I crash into them. In a frenzy I belt out 'Broken Desire' with all the rage and volume my voice box can manage.

> We're rats running round this maze
> Feelings so true must hide
> Deaf, blinded and betrayed
> So you see we both have lied
>
> Desire lay broken on the floor
> There's a stinging in my feet
> That tiger's knocking at my door
> As if to make victory sweet
>
> I panic whenever I see you
> Wondering if maybe this time
> My wounded heart will break through
> And you will read my mind
>
> We're feeding emptiness inside
> With all kinds of additives
> How often have you cried
> You who takes but never gives?

> Desire lay shaken yet still clothed
> In the costume of my choice
> Teasing tiger will not disclose
> If there's a hint of love in my voice

There is no audience applause reverberating through my head this time. I am without illusions, grounded in reality. Returning my guitar to its leaning position against the far corner of my room, I feel that I've succeeded in blasting a good portion of heavy-duty anger out from me. And I did it in a constructive way.

A rush of relief surges through my body like a strong welcome breeze on an intolerably hot summer day. Payback? No. I'll never be like Cynthia or Dan, or anyone like them. I swim in different streams, which includes hopes and fanciful dreams to counteract all the rotten crap in life. I can't divide and conquer; I won't use people for my own selfish purposes. A welcoming fantasy returns to me. Hearing the rush of applause scattering through my head, I smile at being childlike again.

Don't get the wrong idea; I haven't found some happy ending to all this. I can't say I've found "the light." Life's a struggle. In two ways, though, I count myself among the world's fortunate few. First, my family sticks together; I have their support, their love. Second, Andy is still my friend. But I have also discovered important pieces about myself that, of course, were always there. My ability to move on is intact, even after being betrayed by the person I thought was "the one for me." Hopefully I can look at the mistakes I've made all on my own, and prevent similar errors from happening again.

Finally I treasure my empathy. Cynthia faked it for a long time, but ultimately I uncovered her complete failure to feel for other people. I don't know if she can do anything about it or not, but either way I do feel sorry for her. Somebody (I can't remember who it was) said: "Compassion is the foundation upon which all other virtues must be built." I see how significant that quote is, and I agree with it completely!

NOW I DECIDE FOR CERTAIN: I'm not a loser. And that's not what this is about, anyway. Bad and better things are ahead for me, everything always changing. I will hold firm to the quality person I am becoming. I must work hard on making myself more compassionate. I'm not on this planet just for me. Every time I became cold and detached, there's when my troubles got worse. Like I said before, I haven't solved the riddles of the universe. I just have a stronger idea of what I'm made of, that's all.

Lisa and I need to share time together, at this very moment. We might end up not even talking to one other. Fine. She'll know that I'm with her.

Walking down the steps to the living room my shoulders feel lighter, like butterfly wings. I am breaking out of the dark cocoon I wove myself into, getting ready for a new life.

Letting the past go past, I practically levitate.